D1430746

AN AVON BOOK

To Octaviana Esquibel

AVON BOOKS, INC.
1350 Avenue of the Americas
New York, New York 10019

Copyright © 1997 by Rick Collignon
Cover illustration by Michelle Yoder
Inside back cover author photo by Jennifer Ammann
Published by arrangement with MacMurray & Beck
Visit our website at **http://www.AvonBooks.com/Bard**
ISBN: 0-380-73220-3

The MacMurray & Beck edition contained the following Library of Congress Cataloging in Publication Data:

Collignon, Rick, 1948-
  Perdido : a novel / by Rick Collignon.
    p.   cm.
I. Title.
PS3553.0474675P4   1997   96-53857
813'.54—dc21   CIP

First Avon Books Bard Printing: February 1999

BARD TRADEMARK REG. U.S. PAT. OFF. AND IN OTHER COUNTRIES, MARCA REGISTRADA, HECHO EN U.S.A.

Printed in the U.S.A.

OPM 10 9 8 7 6 5 4 3 2 1

"THE NIGGER CAME TO Guadalupe in the summer of the year 1946," Telesfor Ruiz said. It was hot and dry, and the rains that came each summer to Guadalupe and moved black with speed over the valley had not yet arrived. The fields were wet only with water from the ditches, which ran full from the heavy snows the winter before.

He came to Guadalupe from the south. The road was not paved then, and in the spring, when the ground thawed, it was not a road at all but only mud. On that day in July, with no rain, the man walked loosely on the hard-packed adobe, as though that were all he had ever done. He was tall and thin and carried a worn canvas bag over his shoulder. His dark clothes were baggy on his frame and too heavy for the season. The face shadowed beneath his cap was weathered and thick featured. He stared at the ground as he walked, as if he thought it might have something to say, although he was no longer interested in what that might be. At times, he would swing the bag off his shoulder and carry it in his right hand, as he was doing when the first person in Guadalupe saw him—a young boy named Gilfredo Vigil, who was in a field throwing rocks at his grandfather's cows. Gilfredo could see that this man's right arm hung four inches longer than his left and that the skin of his face and hands was black.

Telesfor Ruiz told Will that he remembered the year the nigger came because it was also the year Eduardo Muñoz froze to death near the church and wasn't found until the snow melted in the spring. Eduardo, an old man whose mind had always been like that of a child, lived with his sister. Each morning, Eduardo would walk the long distance from his sister's house to Felix's Café. There, he would sit, drinking coffee by himself, talking to no one, and look out the window at the village. After three cups of coffee, he would rise hurriedly from the table, as though he had heard a voice, and return home. Sometimes, if the café was quiet, Felix García would watch the old man walk down the hill into the valley. Eduardo would walk with his head bent, his arms stiff at his sides, but for an old man, he walked quickly with a purpose no one understood.

On the day Eduardo froze to death, the wind blew harshly from the north. Eduardo stood at the window in his sister's house dressed in rubber boots, watching the January wind blow the snow sideways. He could feel it touch the back of his hand as it came through the cracks around the frame of the glass. When his sister, Lucinda, came from bed an hour later, she found her house empty. By then, her older brother was already dead.

When Eduardo reached the church, only a few hundred yards from Felix's Café, his face was burnt red from the wind and his ears were the color of chalk. Although Eduardo's feet still moved, he was walking in place. The wind inside his clothes pressed on his chest, and his body felt as though it had been taken with fever. He took off his coat and shirt, pulled off his boots, and sat down in the snow. Before him, he could see hundreds of small birds the color of the snow. Each one made a noise just louder than the wind. Eduardo watched them as they hopped onto his legs and sat on his bare feet and crowded together in his lap. After a while, he lay gently on his side, careful not to crush them. He closed his eyes and thought that the sound of these birds was something he had heard before.

Eduardo lay lost in the snow for almost two months. One night in early March, when the weather that winter had finally broken, Father Jerome was returning to the church after visiting Guadalupita García. Guadalupita had been near death for three years and had spent that time praying incessantly in a language not even she knew and summoning the priest to her home. There, Father Jerome would sit by her bed, staring at the white adobe wall and wondering when this old woman, who spoke such strange words, would die and leave him in peace. As he neared the church, he stumbled off the path and into the snow. When he looked up, he saw in the moonlight the half-naked body of Eduardo Muñoz, curled about itself. The old man's eyes were closed, and on his face was a smile.

It was the summer of that year, Telesfor Ruiz told Will, that the nigger came to Guadalupe.

He stayed in Guadalupe for seven years. On the day

he arrived, he walked through the village without a glance about him, and just past Felix's Café he suddenly cut off the road, through the fields to a house near the base of the foothills that had sat empty for more than twenty years. Gilfredo Vigil, distracted from throwing stones at his grandfather's cows, had followed the stranger through the village, trailing far behind as if this man were an animal that he had never seen before and he were unsure whether it could be trusted. Gilfredo stood in the sagebrush and watched the man push open the door of the house and then lower his head and walk inside. Soon after, Gilfredo saw smoke coming from the stovepipe. Only eleven years old and living with too many older sisters, he thought that this village, which had always been the same to him, had changed in a moment.

The nigger's name was Madewell Brown, and he moved into the house that had once belonged to Antonio Montoya, who had long ago left the village. No one in Guadalupe knew how Madewell had come to choose this house, and since he kept to himself and also because most people were uneasy in his presence, this was a question never asked. He lived there as though it were his.

Horacio Medina, who owned many head of cattle and much of the better pasture land in Guadalupe, was the only person to try to start trouble with Madewell Brown. He went to Tito's bar one night in August and bought whiskey for everyone, a thing he was never known to do. Then he said that this village was not a place for someone, especially a nigger, who had appeared from nowhere and moved into the Montoya house as if he owned it, which he didn't. Horacio bought some more whiskey and said that what they should do was walk to Madewell Brown's house and show him what was what.

Alfonso Vigil, who had been in the bar since the day before celebrating the birth of his fourteenth granddaughter, raised his head and in a voice like gravel and with eyes that had turned bleary and red said that if anyone's house should be burned, it should be Horacio Medina's, as it was he who had cheated the people of Guadalupe whenever given the opportunity. And besides, Alfonso went on, it was too late in the evening to go to the nigger's house; they would only disturb him.

In the years that Madewell Brown lived in Guadalupe, the only person to come to know him at all was Felix García. On the first of every month, before dawn, Madewell would walk to the back door of the café and Felix would sell him beans and flour and meat. As Felix too was a man who kept to himself, much of their dealings were done in silence. But on days when the weather was poor, Madewell would duck his head and step inside. Felix would look at this man and wonder how someone like him had come to this place.

Madewell told Felix that although he once had a family, it was now scattered about as if blown. One day he had packed his belongings in his bag and begun walking. He said he had spent his life always moving with others like himself and that, in the end, it had come to nothing. He said he had stopped in Guadalupe because when he first saw the village he thought that it had the feel of having been here forever and would look no different in a hundred years. And also, when he walked down the hill, he could see a small boy in a field running about as if being chased and throwing rocks at cows. Felix, who knew Gilfredo Vigil threw stones at everything from chickens to open windows to his older sisters, thought that if he had seen someone like Gilfredo, it would have been a good reason to keep on walking, not to stop. If it occurred to Felix to ask why Madewell had moved into the house that had once belonged to Antonio Montoya, he never asked. Felix took Madewell's money and gave him food in return, and they stood outside the café each month as though it were something the two of them had done forever.

Madewell Brown became like a shadow living in the village, someone who had moved into its midst from the outside and then closed himself away. He hauled water from the ditch that ran through the field next to his house, and in the winter, he melted snow. Sometimes he would be seen gathering firewood, branches of piñon and cedar, in the foothills. Those who saw him would think of a wild animal that had grown old and moved slowly, no longer concerned about whether it were seen. But for the most part, he stayed inside his house doing no one knew what.

One morning when Madewell Brown came to Felix's Café, he carried his canvas bag and was dressed in the same clothes he had worn when he arrived years ago. It was summer, and the sun had not yet risen. The sky was only pale to the east. When Felix saw him, he knew that this man was leaving Guadalupe and that although he had met with him every month for years, he knew almost nothing about him.

For a moment, neither man spoke. Then Felix, a quiet man with little sense of humor, said he had always thought Madewell was too sensible to take a walk on a day that promised to be so hot. Madewell leaned close to Felix and said he had once been the father of six children who had all come to nothing like himself. He knew their names and their faces, but that was all. He told Felix that when he was born, his father, who worked with his hands and his back and died too early, had given him the name he carried so that what he did in life would go well. Then Madewell Brown said he was leaving Guadalupe now because there was no longer anything here for him. He also said he had left something in his house that he wished Felix to see.

Gilfredo Vigil was the last person in Guadalupe to see Madewell Brown. He was in his grandfather's field irrigating, and he was no longer a young boy but a young man. As he worked the shovel, he watched Madewell walk through the village, up the hill, and out of his sight. Gilfredo thought that this man looked and moved no differently from the first time he had seen him. He could see again how much longer one of Madewell's arms was than the other and thought that he should drop his shovel and run after him and ask why this was so. But he didn't. It wasn't until Gilfredo himself was approaching old age that he woke suddenly one morning with the nigger in his mind and realized that Madewell Brown had spent his life throwing rocks.

After the café closed that day, Felix cleaned the kitchen and wiped the tables. Then he walked up the hill to the house where Madewell had lived. The sun had set, and Felix could feel his shirt, which was moist from the heat in the kitchen, cool against his back. He looked at the house and thought it already felt empty. Felix pushed the door open and stepped inside.

The mud plaster on the walls inside had been painted white, and over that were drawn so many pictures that for a second Felix felt as though the room were crowded. He shut his eyes, and a soft wave of dizziness washed over him. When he opened them again, he began to turn slowly in a circle. All about him were thousands of paintings. They ran from one wall to the other, even across the surface of the door and above the archway that led into another room. They were painted in black, red, yellow, green, and in colors Felix had never seen. In each painting were six children, and from one wall to the next they aged, and as there were so many of these paintings, they seemed to grow old together by the moment.

They were drawn at birth, Telesfor said, lying closely together under one blanket. Their faces were clear and smooth, their eyes wide and surprised. Above them was a black sky with stars and a yellow moon. Felix watched them begin to crawl and then walk clumsily, falling into each other. He saw them in trees and in dry arroyos and in groves of scrub oak, always together, and in a boat on a river that flowed flat and was only water. He saw them kiss each other and wrestle in the dirt and throw rocks at cows and start fires that grew too big. He watched them asleep at dawn and in the rain and in snow without coats or shoes. And at the end, with age, the six of them sat looking out at the person who had drawn them. Felix saw that in this house Madewell Brown had raised his family and that when he left, he left them behind.

It took Telesfor Ruiz a long time to tell this story to Will. By the end, the night had grown dark and Telesfor's voice sounded like air. Will asked him if he had ever seen the paintings and where in Guadalupe this house was. Telesfor answered that he had seen them just once, but he had never gone back because the sight of them alone in the house made him too sad. He told Will that the house Madewell Brown had lived in was no longer standing. A few years after Madewell left, Horacio Medina bought the land for back taxes. Not long after that, he sold it to the mine, which tore the house down. All that remained now were some old fenceposts and broken glass and pieces of adobe with paint.

One

ONE WINTER, WILL
Sawyer found buried in his wall the carved figure of a
Lady. He found her by accident. He was driving a nail
into the adobe wall beside the kitchen stove when the
head of the hammer broke through the thin layer of mud
into air. The hole she stood in was not much larger than
she, narrow and a little over a foot high. She was coated
with dust and mud and woven with spiderwebs as if tied
in place. Her hands came together at her chest; her eyes
looked straight ahead. Her mouth was full and without a
smile. The base she stood upon was a piece of flat cottonwood. Much of the paint on her gown and on the
robe that fell from her head to her feet had peeled away.
Will didn't know who had hidden her in the wall, only
that she had stood there for a long time.

He never told anyone about her, not Felipe, not even
Lisa, and on days like this one he would take her from her
hiding place and stand her on the kitchen table. They
would stay there together without talking, or at least she
wouldn't, and look out the open door. Today, all they could
see was rain and the clouds hanging low on the foothills.

Will had left early that morning with Felipe, an hour or so before dawn, rain falling so softly that they both thought it wouldn't keep up much past sunrise. Felipe drove, their tools in the box in the bed of the pickup, the ladders vibrating on the rack above the cab. The radio was tuned to a Spanish station, and the reception was so poor that to Will it sounded as though the voices came from another world.

They drove through Guadalupe, heading north. Most of the houses were still dark, and this early there wasn't even a sign of life in Felix's Café. The narrow, two-lane highway was empty except for the occasional trucker hauling hay and dragging clouds of vapor in his wake. The rain seemed to be falling harder.

"This might be a bad idea," Felipe said.

Will leaned forward and wiped the fog off the windshield. "How can you even see?" he said. "Maybe if you put on the wipers, we won't hit a cow." Felipe grunted and hit the switch, and the wipers clacked back and forth. "All we got to do," Will went on, "is get some measurements."

"This was your stupid idea to take a job so far away."

"It won't take long," Will said. "We'll give her a price and come home."

"It's a five-hour drive," Felipe said. "Besides, who's going to crawl around her roof in the rain?"

"You think it'll rain all day?"

"It rained all night," Felipe said, as if that had something to do with now. "Even if it doesn't, the roof'll be slick."

Twenty miles north, they turned east onto a gravel road that would take them across the valley and over the Rio Grande. From the river, they still had another good hour of driving. Will leaned back low in the seat and lit a cigarette. He cracked open the window and watched the draft pull the smoke from the cab. He thought that since coming to New Mexico, he had spent half his life in the cab of a truck.

Felipe took his eyes off the road. He could see that Will's head moved with the motion of the truck and that his eyes were closed. "When we get to the bridge," he said, "if it's still raining, we're turning back."

"I'd hate to have to do this again tomorrow," Will said, his eyes still shut.

Felipe grunted and looked back at the road. It was raining harder. "Don't think you're going to sleep on this ride either, jodido," he said.

They had worked together for nine years. For a little while, at the beginning, they had been polite and careful with each other. But now, after so long, it seemed that all they did was argue like viejas. Felipe knew that this was not his doing and wondered how someone as even-tempered as he had come to have two wives who each took a great deal of pleasure in telling him what to do.

"You know why this lady wants a price?" he said. "So she can get her brother or her tío or some other relative to do it for less."

The sky became gray, light enough now that they could see the flatness of the land stretched out between the two mountain ranges, the Sangre de Cristos behind them and to the west the low, barren hills of the San Juans. They drove by some old fence lines and a ruin that was no more than a stone foundation and a pile of rocks that had once been a chimney. Felipe wondered why anyone would choose to live out here, where winter was too long and the wind always blew and nothing grew but sagebrush and sparse grass cropped short by generations of cattle. The road was beginning to rise gradually, and Felipe knew that just over the next hill it would dip down to the river. "Finally," he thought.

Las Manos Bridge spanned maybe eighty feet of river. The Rio Grande hadn't gouged out the terrain here as it had farther south but flowed slow and steady. The bridge was built with heavy steel trestles above and below, the roadway lined with thick planks that jarred loose when a vehicle passed over them. The trestles were dripping with rain; the steel was dull black.

Felipe stopped the truck in the middle of the bridge and shut off the engine. Will could see that Felipe's eyes were bloodshot. From driving, from not enough sleep, from too many beers the night before, he didn't know.

"What do you think?" Felipe asked.

"I think you were right," Will said. "This is a bad idea."

"Now you say that. We can go on if you want."

Will shook his head. "You want to stay here and talk about this, don't you?"

Felipe grinned and then leaned against the truck door, pushing it open. "Eee," he said, "it's probably a sunny day in Guadalupe. The rain sitting out here." He climbed out of the pickup, walked to the edge of the bridge, and began urinating in the river. Out the driver's door past Felipe, Will could see that the river was running high and muddy, rain spitting against the surface. Felipe said something to him in Spanish that he didn't catch.

"My father's neighbor calls this place puente de la niña," Felipe said then, "and he says if you want to fish in the river, fish somewhere else."

Will shook his head and smiled. "I didn't get that," he said.

Once, for two weeks, Felipe had refused to speak anything but Spanish to Will. Both thought this would be a good idea, as Will would thus learn a language spoken by everyone, but after the two weeks had passed, Felipe gave up in frustration. While it was true Will learned the words quickly, it was also true that when he spoke, his speech was so slow and out of cadence that Felipe would close his eyes and smile with feigned patience, wishing his friend would shut up and speak English. He thought there must be a part of Will's brain either underdeveloped or missing altogether.

"I will never understand," Felipe said, "how anyone could be here so long and know so little. Niña is girl, a young girl, but what my father's neighbor means it to be is 'dead girl.'" He zipped up his pants, came back to the truck, and leaned against the cab. His hair was black and wet with rain. His face was a little puffy but clean shaven and deep brown now from the summer.

"Puente is bridge," he went on. "Bridge of the dead girl. Puente de la niña. He found a dead girl, a gringa, out here hanging from one of the beams. So he named this place after her."

Will got out of the pickup and faced Felipe across the hood. The rain was falling heavily enough that he could feel it through his shirt. He looked up at the dark trestles.

"Some white girl hung herself out here?" he said.

Felipe shrugged. "That's what I heard."

Will looked back at him. "Damn," he said. "What a place for her to be. So when did this happen? Yesterday or a long time ago?"

Felipe grimaced and blew air out of his mouth. "Twenty, twenty-five years ago, I think. Maybe a little longer. I was still in school. I forget how old."

"I never heard this story. I've been here a long time, but I never heard this story."

Felipe pushed himself off the side of the pickup. "So?" he said. "You think you should know the whole history of a place after just a few years? Besides, it's just a story, Will. Don't worry about it."

"I'm not worried about it," Will said. "It's just that there's nothing out here." He looked past Felipe. On the west side of the river, the earth was churned up where cattle had come to drink, the river beginning to cut into the clumps of mud, rising with the rain. Beyond that there wasn't much to see. Flat land with sagebrush and a sky that sat low with clouds. He looked up again at the trestles dripping with rain and thought that if he were to close his eyes, he would almost see her.

Felipe straightened up and moved his shoulders back and forth. He ran a hand through his hair, squeezing out the rain so it dripped down the back of his shirt. He shivered and thought that he did not need to catch a cold in July. "It was a long time ago, Will," he said. "Come on, let's get out of here and go home."

They drove back the way they had come. Felipe dropped Will off at his house and then went home. He hoped his children were still asleep and that his wife, Elena, was still in bed and would be happy to see him. Will took the Lady out of the wall and spent the day with her, staring at the rain and thinking about a gringa hanging by herself from Las Manos Bridge.

Telesfor Ruiz, Will Sawyer's only neighbor, died in his bed of old age just a year after Will came to Guadalupe. Telesfor lived in the adobe his father had built, a couple of hundred yards from Will's house. After Telesfor's death, his relatives, who no longer lived in Guadalupe, came and buried him. They emptied his house and his sheds, hauling away even the old man's cookstove. They sold his sheep and three head of cattle to the Medina family. Then they boarded up the two small windows in the house, nailed shut the door, and went back to where they had come from. Will never knew what happened to Telesfor's dog, which was small and twisted with age and no longer barked at anything.

The first time Will met Telesfor, he had been in Guadalupe only a few weeks and knew no one. He had spent that time alone, working on his house and wondering what he was doing in a place where people looked at you as if you weren't there and almost always spoke in a language in which all the words sounded alike. One afternoon, he had walked to Telesfor's house and found the old man sitting on a stool beneath his portal. Telesfor invited him inside for coffee, and they sat awkwardly at the kitchen table for a long time. Finally, as if from nowhere, Telesfor told him that one winter when he was a small boy, the snowfall had been so heavy that all of the roofs in Guadalupe collapsed on the same night. When he woke, he said, there was mud and water in his bed and he could not feel his feet. All he could see above him was falling snow and stars.

When Will walked back home that day, it was sunset, the sky streaked red. The color fell on the mountains and on the sagebrush. In Will's mind was the picture of small boys trapped under mud and snow. He had never heard such a story, and he thought that beneath the village he could see with his eyes was something else. He thought that maybe the next day, after he made sure the roof on his house was sound enough to hold the weight of snow, he would walk back to his neighbor's house.

Across the creek and not far from Telesfor and Will's places was a baseball field with high weeds in the outfield and stones mixed with dirt in the infield. Once each week, the field would be ringed with vehicles and there would be a game, always between the same two teams. For a long time, the noise of engines and of men who had drunk one beer too many bothered Will. But after a while, he got to like it. He liked hearing the kids rushing through the cottonwoods along the creek and the voices of the women calling out to them. Finally, he walked over one night and borrowed a glove and saw what it was like to have a ball fly so far and then fall into his hand.

But Will didn't feel like playing baseball tonight. He felt tired after doing nothing all day but taking a long drive in the rain with Felipe. The clouds had moved out by late afternoon, and the sun had come out in a haze of mist. By then, Will was sitting in a chair against the south side of his house watching the sky grow dark. The voices at the field had quieted down, other than an occasional yell, and he could hear truck engines revving and pulling out.

It was nearly dark when Felipe drove over. His truck pulled into the drive and hit the ruts hard, headlights shooting everywhere. Felipe pulled up and parked alongside the house.

"So," he said, one arm hanging out the open truck window. "I thought you'd be over at the field."

"I didn't make it." Will pushed out of the chair and went over to the pickup. "Who won?"

"I don't know," Felipe said. "I don't keep score. Your girlfriend was there."

"Lisa?"

"Yes, Lisa. How many girlfriends do you have? She asked me where you were. Then she stayed for a little while and left."

Will let out a long breath of air. "I guess I should have walked over," he said.

Before Will, Lisa had been with a friend of Felipe's named Pablo Padilla. On his head the day after he stopped seeing Lisa was a large bandage. Pablo told everyone that he had fallen off his roof and landed in the woodpile, but the story Felipe heard from Elena was that Pablo had called Lisa something he shouldn't have, and when he turned away to drink from his beer, she hit him with a board. Felipe tapped his fingers against the side of the pickup. He thought that if he had a girlfriend like Lisa Segura, it would be dangerous to let her sit by herself at a baseball game and grow angry. He also thought that if Will wasn't smart enough to know this, why should he tell him?

"What time do you want to leave in the morning?" Felipe asked, smiling a little.

"The job's off," Will said. "I called the woman after you dropped me off and gave her a guess over the phone. She said she didn't think it would be that much and since her brother put on shingles once, maybe she'd let him do it."

Felipe grunted. "I told you," he said.

"I'm going to go see Lisa in the morning. After that, maybe I'll come by your house. If you're not doing anything, we could see your father's neighbor." It was dark now. Will could just see Felipe's face through the shadows inside the cab.

"The girl on the bridge," Felipe said. "I should be careful what I say to you."

"It's a good story, Felipe," Will said. "I just want to hear the end of it."

Two

WILL WALKED THROUGH the door of Felix's Café at seven A.M. and the place looked to him as it did every other morning. The same group of regulars was crowded noisily at one table in the middle of the room, and off to the far side, by himself and as still as stone, was Felix García. Felix had suffered a stroke two years earlier, severe enough to prevent his ever again flipping an egg or spitting in the beans, which is what he used to say gave his frijoles their special flavor.

Will had heard that on the morning of Felix's stroke, he and his son, Pepe, were preparing beans with garlic and cilantro when Felix turned to Pepe and, without any expression on his face, said, "Your mother's breasts, hijo, are the reason I cook so well." As Felix had always been a quiet man with little sense of humor and his wife, who had been dead for nine years, had not seemed to possess especially remarkable breasts, what Felix said startled not only Pepe but everyone in Guadalupe when they were told. After saying this, Felix's eyes rolled back in his head and he fell to the kitchen floor, where he lay on his side with his face pressed against the linoleum.

Pepe now cooked alone in the kitchen. Each morning, he would dress his father and they would walk together to the café, where the old man would sit all day by himself. Will no longer came to the café as often as he once did, but when he did, he would glance over at Felix, whose eyes were always open and staring, his shoulders now frail and hunched, and Will would wonder about the last words he had spoken and what was going on now inside the old man's mind.

The conversation at the large table quieted when Will came through the door. About half the men had just come off their shift at the copper mine. The other half were there to talk until the coffee drove them outside to work. Will nodded and then went to their table when Lloyd Romero waved him over. Lloyd took Will's hand and pulled it close to his chest. The man sitting next to Lloyd said good morning and moved his chair over to give Will room.

"Qué pasa, Will?" Lloyd said. "I haven't seen you in a long time." The table was littered with coffee cups. Cigarette butts smoldered in the ashtray. "Where've you been?"

Will knelt down beside the chair, his hand still in Lloyd's. "We've been busy, Lloyd." He looked toward the kitchen. "Did Lisa come in this morning?"

"You get that job across the valley?" Lloyd asked, pulling Will's hand closer to his chest.

"No. It didn't work out. It's too far, anyway. Five hours on the road."

Lloyd looked across the table. In a loud voice he said, "I remember Will the first day he came here. He stops me out on the highway and asks, 'Is this Albuquerque?'" The guys across the table smiled. One of them said, "How's it going, Will?" Will shrugged okay.

"I tell him, 'Yes, this is the outskirts of Albuquerque,'" Lloyd went on, "'the rest of the city is over the hill.'" Lloyd looked back at Will and squeezed his hand. "You remember, no?"

"Yes, Lloyd," Will said and smiled. "I remember."

What he remembered was driving down the highway nearly twenty years ago and running into Lloyd Romero at a gas station. When he asked how far it was to the next town, Lloyd told him to get his ass out of here, that Guadalupe didn't want people like him around. A couple of miles down the road, the engine in Will's truck blew. He had sat on the side of the highway wondering what to do next until finally he walked back to Guadalupe. Eighteen years later, he was still in this village and had come to think he would never leave.

"You know, Lloyd," Will said, pulling his hand free and standing up, "you haven't changed since that first day we met."

Lloyd laughed and put his hand on Will's arm. "You're okay, Will, you know. Come by my house later. We'll drink a few beers." He scraped his chair back and stood up, rattling off a string of Spanish Will didn't understand. The men at the table laughed and then gathered up their cigarettes and hats. They threw some coins on the table, nodded good-bye to Will, and headed out the door.

Will sat down at a table by the window. The sun had not yet risen above the mountains. He looked out on the highway and, beyond that, on most of the village of Guadalupe. The town sat in a small valley, the road rimming it on the west and the Sangre de Cristo mountains to the east. Houses and sheds and old corrals were scattered throughout, and fields of alfalfa were everywhere. The creek ran thick with juniper and cottonwoods through the center of the valley. Smaller ditches branched off it that fed water to the fields. Up close to the foothills, he could make out the flat ground of the baseball field, but the trees just beyond grew too tall for Will to see his house. The town was quiet. There was no breeze to stir up the dust, not much traffic on the highway.

Will heard the kitchen door swing open, and when he looked over he saw Lisa. She was wearing blue jeans and a white blouse tied at the waist instead of tucked in. She began cleaning up the mess at the center table.

"We're closed," she said.

"Lisa," Will said, "I didn't know you'd be at the field. You should have driven over."

She straightened up, a dishrag in her hand. Will could see skin between her shirt and her jeans. "Shit you didn't," she said, pointing the dishrag at him. "I see you there every week. You think I don't have better things to do than sit and smile at a bunch of borrachos with baseball mitts?" She glared at him and then bent over and wiped some more at the table.

Will lit a cigarette. He thought it was good that everyone had left the café. He knew Lisa was not one to be quiet even in a crowd. "Come on," he said. "Sit down. We'll drink some coffee."

Lisa didn't answer. She was throwing cups into a plastic container as if they were made of steel. She gave a final swipe at the table and kicked the chairs back in place. Then she straightened up and stared at Will. "Who needs it?" she said and turned and went back into the kitchen.

Will smoked most of his cigarette before she came back out with a pot of coffee and two cups. She sat down across from him, filled both cups, and slid the pot off to the side.

"I mean it, Will," she said, leaning toward him. "It makes me crazy. All my life I watched my mother. Cooking and cleaning forever. Raising children by herself with my father always gone. And even when he was home, none of us wanted him there. So don't even think this is just a little thing." She leaned back in her chair and picked up her cup, cradling it in her hands. She smiled. "If you do it again, Will, I'll have Mundo shoot you."

Will had met Lisa in the middle of January, the past winter. He had asked her how it was that in a place so small he had never seen her before, and she told him it was just his bad luck. She and her family had lived in Guadalupe forever, and she was not one to hide herself. She told him that she had one brother and that his given name was Joaquín, but everyone in Guadalupe called him Mundo. Will knew who her brother was, and he also knew that he was someone to stay away from. He had heard the stories about Mundo. About the fights that would always start for no reason. The time Mundo had shot at someone for talking wrong and the bullet had ricocheted off a car bumper and struck Mundo in the shoulder. The untold number of truck accidents from which Mundo would crawl away, abandoning the vehicle, and walk back home to Guadalupe. Will had run into him a few times in the years he'd lived here. Even before Will began seeing Lisa, he had always felt a meanness in the air about her brother and also a madness that made Will feel that anything could happen and whatever it was would be unpleasant. He didn't say anything to Lisa when she told him who her brother was. He couldn't see Mundo in her face or in the way she moved. But he had come to find something in her that she shared with her brother, a part that looked at the world one way, and if it was askew, it didn't matter.

It was snowing the morning Will met Lisa, and the roads had not been plowed. He was driving and came across her as she walked home from the café. No one was out but the two of them. He slowed the truck alongside her and rolled down the window to ask if she wanted a ride. Without looking at him, she said, "I know you."

Snow was snaking across the road, and everything was white. Will, who had no idea what this girl was talking about, asked again if she wanted a ride home. She stopped walking and faced him. Her arms were wrapped around her body, and beneath the large wool hat she was wearing, her face was burnt a dark red from the wind. "Are you sure you want to do this?" she asked him.

"Do what?"

She climbed into the truck, and just a little way down the road she took his hand and brought it to her face. He could feel how cold her skin was. "Take me somewhere," she said to him.

Now, she reached forward and put her cup back on the table. "Mundo gets mad when people mess with the family."

"Lisa," Will said, "you'd shoot me yourself before you'd ask your brother."

She laughed and then rose from her chair, leaned across the table, and placed her mouth against his. Will could taste chile and syrup on her breath. "That's right, Will," she said. "I would. So don't do this again." She pulled away and sat back down.

"All right. I'll be careful."

"Good," she said and looked out the window, a half smile on her face. The sun was pushing over the mountains and sunlight was beginning to crowd into the café, snaking its way between the tables and chairs.

"I've got to get going," Will said, sliding his chair back. "I'll see you tonight."

"Maybe," Lisa said, without looking at him. "I'll have to think." She took in a breath of air and let it out slowly. "Okay, I'll see you tonight."

"Good."

"You don't want to eat?"

Will stood up slowly. "I already ate," he said. "Besides, Felipe's waiting for me."

"So go, then. Felipe will complain all day if you're

late. If you see Elena, tell her I got the stuff she wanted."

"What stuff?"

"Stuff," she said. "Drugstore stuff. You need to know everything?" She raised her eyebrows. "Where are you working today?"

"We're not. I'm going to pick Felipe up, and then we're going to see a friend of his father's."

Lisa raised her hand, shielding her face from the sun. "You might get a job in town?"

"No," he said. Felipe and Will hadn't done any work in Guadalupe for three years. Everyone in town did things for themselves. When someone did ask for an estimate to fix an old roof or shore up a portal that was leaning too far, Will figured it must be out of curiosity because they never got the job. They'd talk to somebody on Monday about work, and the next weekend Will would drive through town and see the guy with his family and neighbors having what looked like a party with hammers and saws.

"No," he said again. "It's not about a job. Felipe told me about a girl his father's neighbor found dead out at Las Manos Bridge a long time ago. We thought since we weren't doing anything, we'd go talk to him."

"We?" Lisa said. "Felipe likes to work. He likes to drink beer. He likes to mess around with Elena and fish with his kids. You don't mean 'we.' You mean 'you.'"

Will suddenly felt uncomfortable. The sun coming in the window seemed too warm. He sat back down. "You know this bridge?" he asked. "It's in nowhere. There's nothing out there, and one morning there's a girl hanging from it like she fell from the sky." Lisa stared at him for a few seconds. "So what?" she said.

"What do you mean, so what? I heard the first part of the story and now I want to hear the end. That's all."

"Let me guess," Lisa said. "She was a white girl, wasn't she?"

Will didn't say anything. He looked at her and thought, Yes, she was white. So where's this going? He leaned back in his chair.

"Felipe said she was white," he said. "Why?"

Lisa stood up. She grabbed the cups and the pot. "Why don't you figure that out?" she said.

Three

WILL TOOK THE TURN
off the highway and drove slowly up Felipe's drive. He
kept an eye out for Felipe's kids, who always seemed to
dart out of nowhere with alarming quickness. Felipe and
Elena had three children, all boys from four to eight years
old. They carried the names of each one of Felipe's
grandfathers: Isidro, Octaviano, and Refugio. Names
that, to Will, seemed too large for the boys, who were all
small and looked much like their father, a little thick on
top with legs that could pump like hell.

When Will asked Felipe how it was he had come to
have three grandfathers, Felipe told him that the one who
had once been named Refugio was not really his grandfather but had only thought he was. Long before Felipe was
born, there was some confusion in his family as to who
was who, and according to Felipe's mother, Refugio remained confused throughout his life. Felipe's mother
went on to say that it was no harm if her children wished
to call Refugio their grandfather but that it was not wise
to do so in front of their grandfather Isidro, since even

the mention of Refugio's name brought a blackness into his mind that was not pleasant to be near.

Will pulled up to the house and parked. He could see Felipe standing in the middle of his garden, his boots stained wet with mud, a shovel propped against his arm. Will got out of his truck and walked over to the edge of the garden. "It's quiet," he said.

"The kids are down the hill with their cousins. The garden looks good, doesn't it?" Felipe worked all spring and most of the summer in his garden. He would plant early and then replant when the frost killed everything. He weeded and irrigated diligently, and Elena had once told Will that she had caught her husband talking quietly to these plants as if they had ears. Will thought the garden looked green and sturdy, even if it was too small for July. "Those tomatoes don't look so good," he said.

"Nobody can grow tomatoes in this country," Felipe said, and he used the shovel to move some dirt so the water flowed down a different path. "I'm supposed to get the water Saturday morning," he went on, bent over, working the shovel with the flat side. "I don't know what it's doing here today."

"Maybe a ditch broke up above," Will said.

"Sure. Or maybe Martin just messed up again and thinks today is Saturday."

Martin Gonzáles was the mayordomo who regulated the flow of water from the head ditch to the homes and fields in Felipe's area of the village. Felipe had spent the last two summers complaining bitterly about him. Martin hadn't let enough water out of the ditch, so it never reached Felipe's house. Martin drove his sister to El Paso, telling no one, and didn't come back for three weeks. Martin got drunk on Friday night and slept late into Saturday and Felipe's water showed up at midnight. The worst was when Martin completely forgot to shut off the water and Felipe's infant plants not only drowned but washed down the hill. Whenever Will asked why he and the others on the ditch didn't just get rid of Martin and make someone else mayordomo, Felipe would say, "Who needs the headaches?"

The ditch system had been in Guadalupe for over two hundred years. Ditches crisscrossed the village as if dug by madmen who thought they could defy gravity, which Will often thought they had. Water ran uphill and around corners and through the roots of cottonwoods and across hollowed logs that spanned arroyos. Not much had changed in the last two centuries. In the deep grass outside each house, even on the hottest day, was the sound of running water. No water rights had come with the land Will owned; they'd been sold off years before. Often, he'd walk to the creek and sit and watch the flow of water, feeling an envy that he'd never felt for money.

Felipe made his way out of the garden carefully, mud clinging to his boots. "I'll let the water run a couple more hours," he said and stuck the shovel in the ground. "Let me guess. You still want to go see that guy, don't you?"

"Yes," Will said. "If you're not doing anything."

"You mean if I don't want to do anything." Felipe

looked up at the sky and squinted. "No clouds anywhere," he said. "It's going to get hot. Let me tell Elena. I'll be right out."

Delfino Vigil lived in an old adobe, not much bigger than Will's, set back off the highway a hundred feet or so. The yard was thick with tall grass and weeds and shadowed by sagging cottonwoods and twisted, half-dead apple trees. The house had sunk in on itself with time, the gable ends leaning in tiredly, the center swaybacked. The metal roof was badly rusted, and tar was packed thick on the seams and around the stovepipe.

Will parked behind an old green pickup and shut off the engine.

"Wait here a second," Felipe said. "Let me see if he's home." He went to the door and knocked. When there was no answer, he opened the door a crack and called Delfino's name. After a few seconds, he looked back at Will and shrugged. Then he walked over to the side of the house and around it, out of sight.

Will could hear the soft sound of water running through Delfino's yard, but the weeds were too high for him to see the ditch. He put his head back on the seat and looked at the house. The plaster was cracked badly on the walls, and Will could see dark stains of dirt where rain had run into the cracks and bled the adobe out. There was one small window on the wall facing him. The paint on the frame was long gone and the wood leaned with the rest of the structure. Will closed his eyes for a moment. When he opened them, he saw Felipe waving him over.

The rear of the house looked like the front except that the land was more open. The grass was still high, but the only trees were small apricots along the ditch. There were a couple of outbuildings that had seen better days, better years, and an outhouse that looked like it was still being used. Against one of the sheds was a small, fenced-in area that held six young pigs, all of them grunting, rooting, and shoving at each other with their bodies. Felipe and Delfino were sitting on wooden chairs up against the house, talking in Spanish.

Felipe introduced Will to Delfino, and the two shook hands lightly. He was a small man, far into his seventies. His face was clean shaven, the skin smooth but tight, pressed in on the bones. He wore a baseball cap, and the hair at his temples was white and sparse. Delfino sat forward on his chair, his elbows on his knees. He and Felipe went on talking, Delfino saying "no" loudly every once in a while and jerking his body back in his chair as though Felipe had brought news he hadn't heard before. Will smiled when they did, as if he knew what was going on, but Delfino's Spanish was too guttural for him to understand and Felipe was rushing on so quickly that his words became blurred. Will took his eyes off them and looked out over the fields of alfalfa spreading away from the house. Two horses, dust colored and stone still, stared back at him from farther down the hill.

Finally, Felipe said, "Delfino wants to know why you are interested in this girl."

Delfino's hat was shading his face, and Will could see fine lines running away from his eyes and down his cheeks. His lips didn't quite cover his teeth, which were too large for his mouth and too white to be his own.

"I'm just interested in the story," Will said.

"It was a long time ago," Delfino said to him in English.

"How long?"

Delfino took off his cap and ran his fingers over his scalp. Will could see a few gray bristles, some liver spots, and not much else. "It was in 1968," Delfino said. "In September, before the first frost." He looked at Felipe. "How long is that?"

"A long time," Felipe said. "I was twelve or thirteen. Almost twenty-five years ago."

Delfino shoved his hat back on his head and looked up at Will. "When did you come here?" he asked. "I never seen you before."

"Years ago," Will said. "I live on Marcello Rael's land. Near the baseball field."

Delfino swiveled on the chair and turned toward Felipe. "Es verdad?"

"Oh, sí," Felipe said. "But sometimes Will gets carried away with what he says. He likes to think he was born in Guadalupe."

Delfino snorted and shook his head. "At one time," he said, "my uncle, Tío Mario, owned all that land where that little house is. He was my mother's brother, and he and his neighbor, Telesfor Ruiz, kept cows from the creek all the way to the foothills. Eighty head, maybe more. When my tío died, his son, who was never good for nothing, sold the house and a few acres to Marcello Rael. The rest of the land and all the water he sold to the mine. He sold it all for pennies. For pocket change." Delfino switched to Spanish, speaking rapidly to Felipe. "Cosas cambién, no?" he said.

Felipe laughed softly. "Nothing changes, I don't think. Maybe one of your family will buy it all back from Will."

"Maybe," Will said and smiled. Delfino turned his head and looked at Will as if he were from another planet.

"Where are you from?" he asked.

"Aquí," Will said, and Delfino snorted again.

"So, what do you care about this girl?"

"Porque no?" Will said. "Maybe she was a relative of mine."

"Pues," Delfino said, "she sure wasn't related to me."

"She was a güera," Delfino said to Will, who was squatted down a few yards from where Delfino and Felipe sat. Will could feel the sun through his shirt and against the back of his neck. Delfino squinted beneath the brim of his cap. "She was an Anglo girl. Pale skin, more pale than yours, and her hair was . . ." He looked at Felipe.

"Blond?" Felipe said.

"Yes, blond, and short like she thought she was a boy. If I want to, I can remember this morning very well. None of it has left me, even after so many years. I was a younger man then. In my fifties." Will picked up a small stone and flicked it in the direction of the hog pen. Delfino pointed his chin at him. "How old are you?" he asked.

"Not fifty," Will said.

"You think fifty's old? Wait until you're in your seventies. Fifty is like childhood." He put his hands on his knees and pushed himself out of the chair. "Maybe someday I'll say that about seventy," he said and walked off, stiff legged, around the house. A few seconds later, Will heard the front door of the house slam.

"Why do you insult the man?" Felipe said.

"All I said was that I wasn't fifty."

"You make me bring you here and you call him an old man. Worse, you say he was an old man twenty-five years ago." Felipe closed his eyes and shook his head. "You cabrón, Will."

Will picked up another stone and tossed it gently at him. It bounced off the side of the house, a few inches from Felipe's ear. "I didn't call Delfino an old man," he said. "Sometimes I get tired of all this. Where am I from? How long have I been here? How old am I? You don't have to listen to any of that."

"He knows where I'm from," Felipe said. "And quit with the rocks."

Will stood up and stretched his legs as Delfino came tottering his way around the house. He was carrying three cans of pop still looped together in plastic. He held them out to Will.

"Take one," he said. "They're cold."

Will thanked him and jerked one loose. Delfino pulled a second can free and handed it to Felipe. Then he sat down in his chair and leaned back, resting his head against the adobe wall. He popped open the can, took a long drink, and belched deeply.

"I was on my way to La Prada," Delfino said. "To get potatoes. Back then, the fastest way was north and then west to the river. You crossed that bridge and in one or two hours you were in La Prada." He drank from the can again and turned to look at Felipe. "You know that road, no?"

"We were there yesterday," Felipe said. "Nothing much has changed since I was small, and it's still the fastest way to La Prada."

Delfino shook his head. "Eee, those roads were bad. The holes would get so big we would drive around them until we made a new road." He looked at Will, who sipped at his pop. It was a little colder than warm, but not much. "There was no county to fix them," Delfino went on. "You drove with a shovel always and hoped the rain wouldn't get you. You had to watch out for cows, también. You drove that road slow. It took you a long time to cross that valley if you didn't want to hurt your truck." Delfino raised his pop can to his mouth and finished it off. He belched again and dropped the can to the ground.

"You want another one?" he asked Will.

"No, gracias," Will said. Delfino looked at Felipe, who shook his head.

"I left early that morning," Delfino said. "Before light. You know that road? How it rises before it comes to the river and then dips down to meet it? You don't see the river until you get to it. I was in that old Chevy pickup I used to have. The blue one. You remember? I sold it to Melvin Ortega when his boy finished high school. Maybe seven years ago."

Felipe bent forward and dragged his fingers across the dirt. He picked up something and tossed it aside aimlessly. "Oh, sí," he said. "The one with no bumpers."

"It had bumpers," Delfino said. "It had bumpers when I sold it." He reached up and rubbed the side of his face. "Maybe it didn't," he said.

Will glanced over his shoulder. The pigs lay stretched out on their sides against the cedar posts where there was still some shade. Their hides were dusty and splotched black in places with dirt. They grunted softly, whistling out air. Even from where Will crouched, he could see the flies working the air above the pen. He looked back at Delfino, who was staring straight ahead at the mountains.

"I got to the top of the ridge," he said, "thinking I would stop and take a piss. And I saw her." He looked over at Felipe. "I never seen such a thing. I thought my eyes were playing tricks. I remember wiping my hand on the windshield, like that would make her go away. She looked like a little boy's toy that flew away and got stuck. She looked like she didn't belong there so much that at first I couldn't tell what I was seeing." Delfino turned to Will. "I can still see her very well," he said. "And I'll tell you this, that was the last time I drove that damn road.

"It was light, but there wasn't sun yet. The air was pale. You know how it is early in the morning. I don't know why, but I left the truck parked in the middle of the road at the top of the ridge and I walked down to the river. There wasn't no wind. Some cows eating the grass on the bank of the river. It was quiet, quiet. The cows just chewing and watching me walk down. You could see the rope, how it went around her neck and running up to those . . . those . . . Cómo se dice?"

"Trestles," Felipe said.

"Trestles." Delfino lowered his head, the skin folding on the upper part of his neck. Will could see patches of whiskers, white against his skin, that he'd missed while shaving. Delfino folded his hands in his lap. "She was naked," he said. "She wasn't wearing nothing. Not even any shoes. Her skin was like chalk, it was so white. I walked down that hill like I was walking into some strange painting God had made in the night."

Delfino took off his cap and turned to Felipe, who was staring down at the ground between his feet. "She didn't look dead," he said. "Not like you would have thought. Her eyes were open. Her arms were loose at her sides. Like this," and he dropped both his arms and tilted his head a bit to one side.

Felipe leaned back and blew some air out of his mouth. "Pobrecita," he said.

"Malo, no?" Delfino said. "Eee, you should have seen her. Her face looked like she didn't want to be dead. Like she wanted to open her mouth and say something. And not to the cows, neither. To me. I got to the foot of the bridge and stopped and stared at her, and one of those shitty cows bawled out, and I swear, every hair on my body stood up and danced. I went back up that road backwards, a lot faster than I came down." Delfino stretched out his leg and moved his foot around as if something itched inside his boot.

"I sat in the truck and watched her, waiting for someone to come. After a little while, I saw that she was turning around. Slow, even with no wind. Turning round and round over the river." He bent over awkwardly and picked up a stone. He tossed it up and down a few times and then gave out a loud shriek.

"Damn dogs," he yelled, throwing the rock. "Get away from here."

Will glanced around quickly and saw nothing but the rock bouncing off one of the cedar posts fencing in the pigs.

"Damn dogs," Delfino said again. "Messing around with my pigs. People don't do nothing anymore. Go to work at the mine in their new trucks and can't even keep their dogs tied up." He said something in Spanish to Felipe. Felipe smiled and nodded his head yes, then straightened out his back and stood up slowly.

"Well," Felipe said, "we should go. The water's still running in my garden."

Will stood up and moved his shoulders around to get rid of the tightness. "How long did you wait in your truck?" he asked Delfino.

Delfino looked up at Will as if he had never seen him before. "An hour," he said. "Maybe a little more. Tomás

Pérez from Mesita drove up. We talked some, and then he went to call someone."

"Call who?" Felipe asked.

"I don't know who he called," Delfino said. "All I know is that later the Guadalupe police drove up in that old pickup they used to have and found me asleep in my truck. They banged on the door and told me I could leave. If I was going to go to La Prada to get across the bridge. I told them I'd never drive over that damn bridge again. I started my truck and drove home. Never did get potatoes that winter."

"Who were the cops?" Felipe said.

"Frank Martínez, Frankie Junior's dad. He's dead now. Shot himself in a hunting accident years ago. You remember? He was so drunk he was walking through the woods holding his rifle backwards. He fell into some scrub oak and the gun went off. The other one was Ray Pacheco. He's still here, but he doesn't work no more. You know where he lives, no?"

"Yes," Felipe said, nodding. "Up the canyon."

"Sí," Delfino said. "Up the canyon."

"What was her name?" Will asked.

Delfino shrugged. "How should I know?" he said. "They buried her up on the hill just outside the church cemetery. It's all weeds now. I didn't go to see her buried, but Ray stopped me on the road a few days later and told me they had put up a cross and that she could have been anyone."

Four

HIPOLITO TRUJILLO AND
Francisco Ramírez and Cristóbal García were the first
men to set foot in this valley. It was in autumn before the
first snow. No one knows where they came from or where
they were going, only that they came here and did not
leave.

Telesfor Ruiz told Will these things one afternoon in
August. It had been a hot day with clouds and no rain.
Will had helped Telesfor half drag an old sofa from behind the house, where it was doing no good, Telesfor
said. They dumped it in an arroyo not far away, where it
sat, Will thought, as if in a place it preferred not to be.
When they walked back to the house, they went inside
where it was cool and ate cold meat and chile and drank
milk with a little whiskey.

Hipolito Trujillo and Francisco Ramírez, who were
first cousins, decided they should return to where they
came from for their families and for the family of
Cristóbal García, and Cristóbal should remain here in this
valley so that there would be someone to say this place

was theirs. Cristóbal, who did not enjoy being alone, told Hipolito and Francisco he feared they would become lost in the mountains and wander forever, and where would he be then? Besides, Cristóbal thought, the junipers that grew along the creek looked as old as God and seemed like things that might move around once it grew dark.

It was in late September that Hipolito and Francisco left the valley. They swore to Cristóbal that within a few weeks they would return with his wife and children and that then they could truly begin a life in their own place where their names would be of importance. As Hipolito and Francisco walked through the piñon and up the foothills out of the valley, Cristóbal stood by himself near the creek in grass that came to his waist. He watched them leave and thought that his life would soon be so crowded he would not even have time to think. He was the father of eight children, all girls who looked like him, small with fast movements and a good nature. Just the thought of them with him here in this place pushed Cristóbal's unease away, and he smiled.

Hipolito and Francisco did not return for two years, and by then, their return was of no matter to Cristóbal García. Just five days after he watched them walk out of the valley, it snowed three feet, and days after that, in snow that came to his chest, Cristóbal lost his mind.

For two years, in his insanity, Cristóbal built small houses that were no more than mounds of sticks and mud throughout the valley. He populated the village with people he had known through his life, and he named the place not Guadalupe but Perdido, because Cristóbal had come to think that not only was this valley lost but so was everyone in it.

Living with Cristóbal were seven priests who all argued; his grandparents and parents, who visited him daily; his twelve brothers and sisters; his wife, Ignacia, and eight daughters, whom he greatly enjoyed; and a multitude of others who would appear whenever his mind wandered that way, which was always. Perdido became so full of people, who always made noise, that Cristóbal thought that if he were not already crazy, all those about him would make him so.

It is not known, Telesfor told Will, why it took so long for Hipolito and Francisco to return. But when they did, they found the valley covered with small dwellings that were good for nothing. And in the midst of all this, a man who was no more than rags and bones and who talked to shadows.

Will looked at the old man sitting at the table across from him. He could see chile on Telesfor's mouth. He thought that although Telesfor was built solid and sturdy, there was still a frailty about him. Will knew that the story he had just heard would be almost impossible to know, and he asked the old man how he had come to hear these things.

Telesfor said that he had heard the story as a child. Maybe none of it was true, but he had never forgotten it. He said that over the years things become lost and that this was a story few knew, other than himself. And now Will.

Will drove alone up the canyon. He drove slowly, keeping an eye out for the old red flatbed that Felipe had said was abandoned at the end of Ray Pacheco's drive. The day had turned hot, though it wasn't yet noon. Will drove with the truck windows down. The air vents under the dash were open, kicking up the stale odor of dust. He nearly missed the turn, just catching sight of the rear end of the vehicle sticking out of a clump of weeds. He stopped in the middle of the road, backed up, and turned down Ray's drive.

When Will and Felipe had left Delfino's, Felipe had sat quietly on the passenger's side of the seat, staring out the windshield and thinking this had been no way to spend the morning. Drinking warm soda pop and listening to stories like that. Although he hadn't seen Delfino for some time, and it was good the viejo looked well, Felipe thought that he could have been fishing or fixing his rotten plumbing or just sitting in the grass beside his garden.

When they got to Felipe's house, Will said, "I don't suppose you'd be interested in taking a ride to Ray Pacheco's."

Felipe didn't turn his head. He could see that the front door of his house was wide open and that piled in front of it were at least seven bikes. He knew his children and their cousins and who knew who else were inside making egg sandwiches and driving Elena crazy and that soon he would hear about it. He wondered how this day, which had begun so pleasantly, had slipped out of his hands. After a few seconds, he asked, "Why do you want to see Ray?"

"I don't know," Will said. "That's where Delfino ended. Why not?"

"Ray's not like Delfino, that's why not."

"No one's like Delfino."

"I don't mean it that way," Felipe said, wondering why he was even having this conversation. "I mean you're not going to get any soda pop at Ray's."

"I'll just ask him what happened," Will said, "and that'll be that."

Felipe shook his head. "Eee," he said, "you don't listen to anything, do you?" He climbed out of the truck and told Will how to find Ray's house. As Will was leaving, he saw a herd of kids run out of Felipe's house. Over their voices, he heard Felipe yell, "And don't let him know you know me."

Ray's place was about a quarter mile off the road. Each side of the narrow drive leading to it was lined by an old cedar fence, and spreading away from it in both directions was alfalfa, thigh high and in need of cutting. The house sat on a couple of acres. Sod, browned out and clipped short, lay along the front. Everything else was dirt mixed with gravel. The house was a long, wood-framed rectangle painted white. Will knew if he dug into the siding, he'd find the aluminum walls of a trailer underneath. A new blue pickup and a small car were parked in front. He pulled in next to the truck and shut off the engine. He took out a cigarette and lit it.

Will smoked and stared at the house, waiting for some sign of life. There wasn't much to see. The yard was neat, nothing lying around. The curtains were drawn and the windows were shut, even on such a hot day. There was an empty feel about the place, as though whoever lived there didn't come out much or else never went in. He thought that maybe Felipe was right, that this wasn't such a good idea, and that if he were smart he'd back up his truck and drive away. He brought the cigarette to his mouth. He could feel the sun lying on his legs. He remembered Delfino saying that the girl looked like a painting God had made in the night, and he thought, What the hell, there's nothing to lose. He hit the horn lightly and climbed out of the cab.

The front door swung open and Ray walked out. Will had seen the man around town for years but had never known his name. They'd never spoken, a nod now and then at the lumberyard or the post office, that was about it. Ray was a large man, in his late fifties or early sixties. He was built thick, but not much of it appeared to be fat. He walked over to where Will was standing and offered his hand.

"Ray Pacheco," he said. They looked at each other for a second, and then Ray moved his eyes away and stared out at his alfalfa.

"My name's Will Sawyer," Will said, turning with Ray to look at the field. Will could see patches of dirt and areas of stunted alfalfa where irrigation water hadn't reached. Blue blossoms puffed out the tops of the plants.

"Almost time to cut," Will said.

Ray looked at him. "It's that time of year," he said. He was wearing a tractor cap pulled down low on his forehead. His face was smooth and dark and heavy, with dark rings beneath his eyes. "What can I do for you?"

There was little doubt in Will's mind that this man would prefer he left and that if he had any sense, he'd ask about buying the old truck parked at the end of Ray's drive. They could kick that around for a few minutes and Will could get out of there gracefully. Instead, he bent down and picked up a stone. He tossed it up and down a few times and then flung it off to the side.

"I work with Felipe Griego," he said. "Yesterday we took a ride out to Las Manos Bridge, and he told me about a girl found hanging out there. I guess this was back when you were a police officer. I thought if you had some time, you could tell me some more about it."

Ray turned his face toward Will. One of his hands moved up to just above his belt, and his fingers began massaging his belly as if he were trying to work out a cramp. He was an inch or two shorter than Will, but with his girth it didn't seem that way.

"Why would he say that?" Ray asked, and Will thought that it wasn't hard to see what kind of police officer Ray had been.

"Why would he say what? About the girl?"

"No," Ray said. "To see me about it. Why did Felipe send you here?"

"Well," Will said, "it wasn't really Felipe. Felipe just told me about the girl. Delfino Vigil told us it was you and Frank Martínez who came out and got the body."

The door to the house opened and an older woman walked out carrying an armful of stuffed animals. She took the steps slowly and walked by Ray and Will without a word. She opened the door to the car, threw the stuffed animals into the front seat, and climbed in after them. She started the engine and drove off, a cloud of dust following her.

"You talked to Delfino about this?"

"Yes." Will took his cigarettes out of his pocket and offered the pack to Ray. Ray didn't even look at them. "I don't mean to bother you," Will went on, "the story just kind of hit me. This girl hanging out there like she fell from the sky."

"She didn't fall from the sky," Ray said. "She was a suicide."

"Is that what the autopsy said?"

"I don't know about any autopsy."

"Who was she?" Will asked. "How'd she get out there?"

Ray looked past him, somewhere else. "It was a long time ago," he said. "I remember it was a suicide. She hanged herself. Why would I care about this? If Delfino said something different, that's his business." He looked at Will. "I got things to do. Don't come back here again." He turned and walked to the house. Will watched the screen door slam behind him.

Five dead skunks lay on the highway in front of the Guadalupe lumberyard. Two of them had been badly mangled by cars. The other three were intact, and Will thought they looked as though they'd keeled over in midstep. The place was quiet and empty, with just a couple of vehicles parked way off to the side that belonged to Joe and his brother Lawrence. The air outside the building smelled rank. Lawrence was behind the front counter when Will walked in.

"What's with the skunks?" he asked.

Lawrence was leafing through a trade magazine. "Keep the door closed," he said without looking up. "It's bad out there."

"It's bad in here," Will said and pushed the door shut with his foot.

"Not as bad as before. It's worse early in the morning, but then you get used to it." He flipped quickly through the pages of the magazine. Lawrence was nineteen years old and was the second youngest of eight brothers who all worked, off and on, at the store. The business had been run by their father and before that their grandfather, who had bought it for too much money from the Medina family. Lawrence tossed the magazine aside and reached for another one. He spent from seven-thirty in the morning to five in the afternoon behind the front desk reading hardware literature and making lists of what to order that Joe always ignored.

"So," Will said. "What were you, attacked?"

Lawrence studied the catalog in his hands and then

swiveled on his stool and tossed it in the trash. "We borrowed a trap from Lloyd," he said. "Been catching a skunk a day all week." He straightened out his back and stretched. "It's too hot to work today. What do you want, anyway?"

"You're trapping skunks, then bringing them over here and running them over?"

"Did you come over here just to bother me?" Lawrence asked. "They're from the yard. From under the building."

The lumberyard had always been infested with skunks. Even in the dead months of winter, you could catch the faint odor of skunk wafting up from the floorboards. One spring a few years back, Julián, the youngest brother, who must have been all of twelve years old at the time, had come up with the idea of gassing them. He and Lawrence had hooked up the exhaust pipe of their delivery truck to a long hose and pumped the fumes under the foundation. They all thought this was a great idea until everyone inside began to get headaches.

"How do you get the skunk out of the trap without getting sprayed?" Will asked.

"The skunk can't lift his tail in the trap," Lawrence told him. "We drag the trap out to the road and open it. The skunk runs like hell and Julián shoots it."

They looked at each other for a few seconds without saying anything. Finally, Will asked, "Where's Joe?"

"In the office."

Joe was laid out in the chair behind his desk, his hands wrapped around the back of his head, his legs stretched out to the side. "Qué pasa, Will?" he said.

Will pulled a chair out from against the wall and sat down. "Not much," he said smiling. "So why is the highway littered with the dead?"

Joe rocked his chair back and forth gently. "Nasty out there, isn't it?"

"Maybe you ought to at least shovel them off the road, Joe. There's people around here these days who might question the massacre of small animals."

"If I leave them out there, it's a warning to the other skunks," Joe said. "Besides, we're getting a good crowd every morning. If the supply holds out, we can sell tickets." He pushed himself forward in the chair with some effort. His fingers played with the papers on his desk. "So how come you're not working?"

Will shrugged. "We had a job fall through. We've got a deck to build next week, so we're taking a long weekend." For a few seconds neither one of them spoke, and then Will asked, "Anyway, you still got that redwood out in the yard?"

"It's sitting out there aging."

"Good," Will said and stood up. "Save me about five hundred square feet, will you?"

Joe nodded, and as Will turned to go, he said, "What's the story with Ray?"

Will went back to his chair and sat down. "Ray who?" he said.

Joe shook his head and then raised his hand, palm out. "Forget I asked," he said. "You know your own business."

"No, I didn't mean it that way. Tell me. Felipe came in here shooting off his mouth, didn't he?"

Joe shrugged. "I asked him where you were. He said you were trying to solve a crime. That you went to interrogate Ray Pacheco."

"Damn," Will said. "Felipe's like an old woman. You ever notice?"

"What I've noticed," Joe said, "is that old women like to hang out with other old women." He looked out the doorway. An old man, his face unshaven and drawn, stuck his head in the office door. He glanced at Will and then asked Joe if he had any gaskets to fix a leaking toilet. Joe told him to look by the hinges and if he couldn't find them to ask Lawrence.

Joe looked back at Will. "How was it with Ray?"

"Not real good."

Joe snorted. "Ray was the village cop when I was growing up. What you see is all there is. He can handle the straightaways, but if he has to turn, get out of the road." The phone on Joe's desk began to ring. Both of them looked at it until Lawrence answered it up front.

"Did Felipe tell you we went to see Delfino Vigil?"

"He didn't use the word 'we,'" Joe said and smiled. The fingers on one hand drummed the top of the desk.

"Tell me," Will said, "how are you related to Delfino?"

"What, because we're both Vigils? We're not related. Maybe a long time ago. Maybe Delfino's my father's fourth cousin or something. Everyone in this town is related if you go back far enough. You know that." Joe leaned forward over the desk. "Anyway," he went on, "I just thought I should tell you to be careful."

"Careful? All I did was ask some questions."

"Will," Joe said, "you can ask Delfino questions and everyone bullshits and has a good time. But when you go see Ray Pacheco, that's something else."

"Delfino's story ended with Ray. So I went to see Ray. There's this girl hanging out in nowhere; wouldn't this interest you?"

"No," Joe said, and Will could tell he meant it. "I have enough problems with the living. I have enough problems with just the skunks. I don't need to mess around with things like this. Besides, it happened a long time ago. This girl's already turned to dirt, Will. Guadalupe's a small town. If this was someone else, you'd tell them to mind their own damn business." Joe leaned back in his chair. "You think Ray thought you were just curious?"

"Have you ever heard this story?" Will asked.

Joe let out a long breath of air. "No," he said and looked at his watch. "You want to go eat? I'll buy you lunch."

"No," Will said as he stood up. "I better get going."

"I didn't mean to ruin your day," Joe said. "If you want to annoy people where you won't get in any trouble, why don't you go up to Canto Rodado? That's where all the old hippies live. The girl was white, Will, wasn't she?"

Will drove north with the windows rolled down, the draft pulling the sour stench of skunk out of the cab. He slowed down in front of Felix's Café and pulled in.

Inside the café, Felix was sitting, as always, by himself near the jukebox, his head bent low and nodding not far from the surface of the table. No one else was in the room. Will walked into the back, where he found Pepe at the stove mixing together a large pile of potatoes and ground beef. On a shelf above the stove was a small radio playing accordion music.

"Pepe," Will said, "where's Lisa?"

"Is anyone out there?" Pepe said without looking up.

"Just your father." Pepe scraped the pile of food off to the side and sprinkled it with massive amounts of red chile powder. "Where's Lisa?" Will asked again.

"Outside on break."

Will looked at the food. The kitchen smelled of garlic and grease and chile. "Make me a couple of burritos, would you?"

Pepe nodded. "Tell Lisa I need her to run to the store."

The air was cool outside after the closed-in heat of the kitchen. Lisa was squatting some twenty yards away in the shade of a large juniper tree, smoking a cigarette, her back to him. She smoked with an easy discipline Will envied. Two or maybe three cigarettes a day. Just to think, she had once told Will, and just enough smoke to keep her lungs strong.

"Hey," Will said.

She glanced over her shoulder. "Hey yourself," she answered and turned her head away.

"Pepe wants you."

Will heard her grunt and watched her stub out her cigarette. She rose with a sigh and walked toward him.

"What time do you get off?" Will asked.

"I'm not in a good mood, Will," she said. She stopped in front of him, the top of her head coming to his chin.

"Let's take a ride later."

"Where?"

"I want to see someone in Canto Rodado."

She looked at him for a few seconds and then said, "I'm covering for Carla until five. Come and get me at six." She brushed by him and then turned back. "You better not be late," she said.

Five

"I'VE LIVED IN THIS village a long time," Will said, "and nobody has ever told me to be careful before." He was sitting alone in his kitchen, his legs stretched out, his hands folded across his stomach. He'd been sitting this way for some time, and it occurred to him that he should check the clock by the stove or he would end up late meeting Lisa. Then there would truly be something to worry about. He hummed out a soft breath of air and closed his eyes.

What Will said was true. He had always been blessed with the ability to slide into the background with a nod, believing it is better to be quiet than to have people look at you. What that got him was a place at Lloyd Romero's table for breakfast, a couple of beers at the lumberyard after work, waves from people who drove by him. What it got him was a home. And now, for what seemed to be no reason, he had pissed off Ray Pacheco and Joe Vigil was warning him to be careful.

Will turned his head and looked at the Lady standing on the table not far from where he sat. "Where did you come from, anyway?" he asked her. He touched the base she stood upon and could feel small indentations in the wood as if someone had once rubbed their fingers there over and over. He knew she was a santo of Our Lady of Guadalupe and that someone who had once lived in his house had placed her in the adobe wall and then covered the opening with a thin layer of mud. She had been there when Will moved in, listening. It wasn't until a year ago, when Will thought he would hang a calendar next to the stove, that he had found her. Now he turned her a little so that she looked out the open door.

"How does a girl not from this place," he said, "end up hanging from a bridge?" Will closed his eyes again, realizing not only that he was talking to a piece of wood, but that he had been doing so for some time.

Lisa's mother lived in a large, unkempt adobe, the exterior plaster pitted and painted a lime green. The yard was cluttered with old sheds jammed full of junk, broken-down trucks, rusted farm machinery that was made to be pulled by horses, and piles of warped gray lumber no one had bothered to clean up since the death of Lisa's father years before. Every so often, Mundo would scavenge some piece of bent, twisted metal and make off with it as if it were some precious artifact. With its curtained windows and the high weeds that grew everywhere, the house looked as though it had been left behind a long time ago.

Lisa lived in a small trailer not far from the house,

where the debris hadn't gathered. A few years earlier, she had painted over the faded aluminum siding. To neaten things up, she had told Will. Not long after, the brown paint had curled away from the walls, making the small, round trailer look like the head of a prehistoric man. She grew corn just outside her front door. The stalks were light yellow and spindly and just ankle high. When Will would tease her about the pathetic state of her garden so far into the summer, she'd tell him, "So what. I don't grow it for food. I grow corn to hear the wind rattle it in the winter."

Will didn't see anyone around when he drove up to the house. Lisa's small, beat-up car and her mother's pickup were parked side by side. He got out of his truck, walked to the house, and knocked on the door. A muffled voice from inside yelled for him to come in.

The door opened into the kitchen, a dark room with one small window facing north that seemed to let in only shadows. The ceiling light, which was centered in the room and strung down from gray aspen latillas, was on. Lisa's mother and Mundo sat at the kitchen table.

Will nodded and said hello. Mrs. Segura nodded back and dropped her head. Mundo didn't say a word. Will always had a difficult time talking to Mrs. Segura. Their relationship was limited to nods. She was in her late fifties but seemed much older. Her gray hair was knotted tightly in back, and her posture was stooped. She was bone thin, and the wrinkles in her face had not come from smiling. She kept busy whenever Will was around, constantly moving, her eyes never near him. Will didn't know how to breach the silence, and he knew she was relieved when he left. Lisa's presence would ease things, but even then, Mrs. Segura would ignore him and speak only to her daughter.

Mrs. Segura rose from the table and went to the sink. She moved some plates around and then walked out of the room. Mundo pushed out her chair with his foot. "Sientate," he said.

Will walked across the room and sat down. C'mon, Lisa, he thought. He couldn't hear a sound in the house and wondered if everyone had gone out the back way.

"I didn't see your truck," Will said.

Mundo leaned back in his chair, one arm stretched out loosely on the table. "Qué quieres con mi hermana?" he said.

Will looked past him out the window. He could see a small dog, not much older than a puppy, tied to a piñon tree. It had worked the chain around the tree so there were only a couple of feet of slack. The dog looked hot and tired and beat, almost as if it knew tomorrow wouldn't be much better. Will looked back at Mundo. "Why?" he asked.

Mundo was older than his sister, closer to Will's age. His hair was dark brown and thinning. It lay flat on his scalp and fell to his shoulders. His face was dark from the sun. His forehead and left cheek were marked with the pale streaks of old injuries. He was built thin, and even though Mundo was sitting, Will could feel a tautness in him that was not far beneath the surface.

"Because," Mundo said, "I don't want you around

here anymore. I don't want you with my sister. You understand?"

Will could see that the lobe of Mundo's right ear was missing. He realized that in just one day two people had told him to never show his face again. He also realized it was only six o'clock. Plenty of time yet for things to get even worse.

"Your sister's not a child," Will said.

"My sister doesn't think, jodido," Mundo said. "But I do. I won't tell you this too many times. Besides, even my mother says you bother her."

"I bother Lisa?"

"You bother my mother," Mundo said, and he jerked his head up slightly. "You come here. You don't talk. You don't do nothing. Take my sister off somewhere. What do you think we are?"

Lisa walked into the kitchen. She crossed the room quickly with long strides and went to the sink. She turned on the tap and rinsed her hands. As Will watched her, he could feel Mundo's eyes on the side of his face.

"You ready?" she asked.

Will stood up slowly. "Yes," he said.

Lisa turned around, drying her hands on the front of her jeans. "Joaquín," she said, "you mind your own business."

"This is my business."

"Oh, I see," Lisa said. She put her hands on her hips and leaned toward her brother. "You think it's fun to mess with this, don't you? Lisa needs her big brother's help. Well, like hell I do."

Mundo waved a hand at her. "I'm not messing with you," he said. "I'm messing with him."

Lisa pointed at him. "You better watch it," she said and then looked at Will. "Let's go."

Canto Rodado had a history, and most of it was recent. Some of it Will knew firsthand; the rest was gossip, picked up at the lumberyard or at Felix's Café over cigarettes and coffee. Before the 1960s, Canto Rodado was a seven-mile wooded slope that butted up to the base of the mountains. The country was empty then, except for a few adobes that were no more than eroded bricks no one remembered much of anything about. A few head of cattle were pastured out on the lower land, and the country higher up was used for hunting deer and fishing the small creeks and cutting juniper for fenceposts.

Will had never seen Canto Rodado the way it once was. He came later, after it had been bought and settled by people from other places. All he knew of it was what he heard back then, how the area was being shut off, how you couldn't hunt without running into a house or a fence or a closed gate. And that was years ago. Now, Guadalupe had given up any thought that Canto Rodado was a relation. It was a place their grandfathers had once owned, a place that had changed hands. And that was that.

Lloyd Romero had told Will a long time ago, "We ran those chingaderas out of here. We just didn't follow them far enough down the road." Will had listened and nodded and never asked him the obvious. If no one wanted these people around, how come they were sold land?

It was Joe Vigil who answered his question. "I was pretty young then," Joe had said, shrugging, "but I remember my father saying that for a bunch of long-haired, barefoot, sulky people, they sure had a lot of money. Guadalupe's no different from anywhere else, Will. We just complain about it longer."

Will had missed those years. Not long after he came to Guadalupe, Canto Rodado started getting cut up and sold into parcels, and the teepees and plywood shacks became relics, almost like the old adobes.

Lisa spit out the truck window. Both her feet were planted up on the dashboard, her body slumped down in the seat. She had to twist her upper body toward the open window and kind of throw the saliva out of her mouth. She fell back heavily against the seat. A can of beer was stuck between her legs.

"Mundo hates your guts," she said, taking a sip of beer.

It was a little past six o'clock. The sun was still hot but slowly inching its way down to the west. The light was not as harsh, making the mountains and foothills seem soft and full. Will drove with one hand, his left arm dangling out the window, playing with the wind.

"I thought you told me he hated everyone," he said.

"He has his pets."

"It's good I'm such close friends with his sister." A truck passed by and the driver raised up a finger in greeting. Will jerked his hand up and waved back. "Has he always been like this?"

Lisa pushed herself up with her feet. She took a long swallow of beer and then belched softly, her cheeks puffing out. "Yes," she said, "he was always like this. Even when he was little. This is something my mother never forgave herself for."

Will glanced over at Lisa and then looked back at the road. "Why would your mother feel that way?"

"Because of how she gave birth to him," Lisa said.

Will held his arm straight up outside the window, the wind pushing against his palm.

"You want another beer?" Lisa asked.

Will hefted the beer in his lap. It was half full and felt warm. "No," he said, "I'm okay. There was a problem with Mundo's birth?"

"There was an accident," Lisa said.

Will looked out at the valley. Miles of pale green sagebrush and in the middle of it, invisible from the road, was the river. He glanced over at Lisa. She was looking at him and smiling.

"Mundo had his first accident at birth?" he said.

Lisa nodded slowly, still smiling. "Do you want to hear the story?"

"Yes."

"It wasn't really my mother's fault. It was the fault of the midwife."

"Ah," Will said.

"When my mother went into labor, my father went to get the midwife, who did not live far. This midwife was an old, old woman. Too old, my mother told me years later. She would forget things. She would forget her name, which was García. Forget where she was going. Sometimes even forget to put on clothes. Her son, who was himself an old man, brought her to our house so she wouldn't get lost. He and my father stayed out in the other room drinking whiskey until they both passed out." Lisa finished off her beer and threw the can out the window. She got another one out of the six-pack, popped it open, and sipped the foam off the top.

"My mother said that everything would have been fine if it wasn't for the midwife. Poor little Joaquín would have been born normal. The birth was going fine at first. The baby dropped from," Lisa put her hand flat on her belly, "here," and she lowered her hand, "to here, and then Joaquín got stuck. He wouldn't budge. He stayed there forever like he was holding on for dear life. The midwife began screaming at my mother. She pushed with both her hands on my mother's stomach. She made my mother stand on the bed and then jump down on the floor to get the baby loose. Nothing. Finally, my mother was on her back on the bed, exhausted, so tired, and the midwife whispered in her old, old voice, 'Hija, if your baby does not come out now, this minute, it will be born muerto. The baby will come from you dead and black.' So my mother, in so much fear, clenched her whole body and pushed with all her might. She pushed so hard that Joaquín became dislodged and flew out of her across the room, hitting his head on the plaster wall. The midwife screamed that my mother had given birth to a bat, and she ran from the room and out of the house. Little Joaquín, pobrecito, nearly died. He lay without even a whimper for weeks with the front of his head smashed in flat." Lisa took a small sip of beer. "My mother said that when it was my time, she was very careful and would not let this old woman anywhere near our house. So you see."

Will looked at her so long the truck drifted into the other lane. "Cuidado," Lisa said.

He swung the truck back gently. The highway was empty. "I've never heard anything quite like that," Will said.

"I know. It's a sad story."

Will turned east just past a small sign that read "Canto Rodado" and onto a wide, well-kept gravel road. He had emptied his beer out the window and was working on a second one that was as flat as the first and not much colder. Lisa was slumped back down in her seat, smoking a cigarette and working on her third beer. Will had never seen her drink more than two and had never seen her drink this fast.

He could see the roofs of houses buried in the woods, steep-pitched with shingles, and, occasionally, the bright glare of the sun off metal. Narrow dirt roads branched off the main one that he knew meandered through the area, with driveways branching off them.

"We used to come up here and pick piñon when I was little," Lisa said. "Whole families all through these woods." She pointed out the windshield. "Gooseberries and rosehips up there where the creek runs."

"When were you up here last?"

She let out a long, tired breath. "Oh," she said, "not since then. There was nothing here. Just this one road and some old trails higher up."

The road swung hard right. Will downshifted to second and took the turn. The road became narrower, lined with tall, thick cottonwoods on the west side that shut out the sun. Higher up, the hillside was dotted with houses.

"You know all these people, Will?"

"No," he said. "Just this guy where we're going. I worked on some of these houses, before me and Felipe got together, but they've probably all changed hands since then."

He turned off the road and headed west up the hill. The road grew rockier, one side arroyoed out where rainwater channeled down the hill. Lisa sat up a little straighter.

"Where are we going?" she asked.

"It's just a little further."

Lisa grunted and then said, "Does this have anything to do with Ray Pacheco?"

The truck lurched over a rock. Will threw the truck into first gear. "How did you hear about Ray Pacheco?"

"I heard you went to his house and gave him a bad time."

Will shook his head. "Who told you that?"

"Lloyd came in and told Pepe, and Pepe told me. Besides, who cares how I found out? It's true, isn't it?"

Will didn't say anything. He kept driving slowly up the hill, the truck creeping through the ruts. Lisa looked out her side window. Finally, she made a ticking noise with her tongue and turned back to him.

"Why are you so stupid all of a sudden?" she said, her voice tight. "What did you think would happen? If you pee behind a bush in Guadalupe, half the town will see you, and they'll go tell the rest. And here you are running around asking questions about some white girl like there's a big secret. What makes me mad is you only care because she's white. If it had been a local girl, you would have listened to Felipe's story and then asked him where the fish were biting."

Will kept quiet, listening to her as she went on. "It's true, Will. And now you got me with you to bother these people who don't want to hear about it either."

He drove a little farther and then stopped the truck in the middle of the road. He could hear some jays clacking away in the woods. A mouse skittered across the road in front of the truck. Hurry, he thought. He looked at Lisa. Her face was flushed. She took a sip of beer, her eyes dark and staring.

"Lisa," he said, "I don't know if it would have made a difference if she wasn't white. If it had been a girl from here, her family would have claimed her and it would have been something everyone knew. But this is different. This girl was by herself in a place where she didn't belong."

"Like you?"

Will didn't even know what she meant by that. He leaned back against the truck door, wondering how something that had seemed so simple had gotten out of hand. "There's no mystery here, Lisa," he said. "It's just a story I wanted to hear. That's all."

"A story?" she said and leaned toward him. "You think this is just a story? Do you know where you live? How do you think it makes people feel to have you come around asking questions about some white girl?"

Will shut his eyes for a second. When he opened them, he said, "I don't know how it makes people feel." He thought that whatever they were talking about had gone somewhere else.

"Are you that bored you have to put your nose in this?" Lisa stared at him, her head cocked a little to one side. "I don't like this, Will. It seems nasty to me. You just better be careful." She looked away, out the windshield. "Let's go," she said, "if we're going to go."

The road dead-ended at Henry Pearson's house another half mile up. The last stretch of road had been so bad that the frame of the truck groaned and the temperature gauge on the panel read hotter than it should. Henry's old flatbed was parked in the shadows under an enormous pine, the back of the truck loaded with fifty-gallon drums spilling over with garbage. Beyond the flatbed was Henry's house. He'd started building the place more than two decades ago, and it looked as if he hadn't learned much as he went along. It was a series of low, one-room add-ons built out of scavenged materials.

Not one of the rooms fit square to the others or even appeared to have been constructed by the same person. It was as if someone had given a hammer and a saw and a bunch of lumber to a gang of kids.

Lisa took a long look at the house. "This is one of those hippie houses, isn't it?" she said.

Will shut off the truck. The engine made a soft clicking noise. "I think we're way beyond hippie here," he told her. He swung open the truck door. "Let's see if he's around."

A large wooden deck covered the ground in front of the house. By the feel of the planks, Will knew they were rotting from beneath. An old power spool lay in the center of the deck, five blocks of cottonwood around it for chairs. Will knocked on the door while Lisa looked about her as if she'd just gotten off the bus from civilization.

Will could hear some muffled movements from inside. A few moments later, the door opened. Henry Pearson was a tall, thin man who looked like he hadn't eaten well, ever. His eyes were deep set and black with deep lines branching out and down from the corners. His hair was thinning and grayer than Will remembered. A full beard covered most of his face, black streaked with white, most of it twisted and knotted up. He was wearing new blue jeans and a white T-shirt that was too small.

"Will," he said, but his eyes weren't on Will. They were on Lisa, who was standing at the far edge of the deck, her back to them. She was looking out at the valley, her hands on her hips.

"Hello, Henry," Will said. "How's it going?"

Pearson shrugged slightly. "The same," he said.

Lisa let out a long breath of air. "It's beautiful here," she said and walked over to them. She swung her arm through Will's. "I'm Lisa Segura," she said and smiled. "So, how do you get out of here in the winter? And why is that road so rotten?"

Pearson's mouth opened and then closed as if the questions were too much for him. "The road keeps people out," he said finally. "And I got a truck that can handle the snow. It never gets as bad as you'd think, anyway."

Lisa made a soft humming sound and said, "It must be nice. No one to bother you. My whole family lives almost next to me. Their noses are always in my business."

Pearson looked down at her for what seemed a long time. He moved his eyes to Will and seemed surprised to realize Will was still around.

"You guys want a beer?" he asked.

Lisa said no, she better not. Will nodded his head yes. When Pearson went into the house, Lisa said, "Does that man look crazy to you?" She looked back out at the valley. "I wouldn't live here if I was dead."

They sat at the spool drinking beer. Pearson's long frame was hunched over, his butt on the edge of the log end, his elbows on the top of the table. Will didn't really know Henry well. They had worked together on job sites years ago, but even then, Henry had never been around very long. He had a tendency to burn out quickly, and after a month or so he'd take his last paycheck, stock up on groceries, and disappear back up into the mountains. Will had been to his house once before, but for the life of him, he couldn't recall why. If Henry got by on the money he earned working, it was a pretty thin existence.

The sun rested at the tip of the San Juan Mountains, casting a dark red glaze that spread across the sky and onto the slopes of the mountains to the east. Lisa sat close to Will, and whenever he put down his beer, she'd slide it to her and take a small sip.

"So," Henry said, "what do you want, Will?"

Will could feel Lisa's eyes on the side of his face. He suddenly wondered why he had brought her up to this place. He was beginning to feel foolish and wished she had stayed in the truck. "I heard a story the other day," he said, "about a girl found dead out at Las Manos Bridge twenty-five years ago. I asked around Guadalupe and somebody told me that maybe she came from up here."

"You drove up here to ask me?"

"Yes."

Henry's hand went to his face, and he began absently stroking the knots out of his beard. "Jesus, Will," he said. "That was a long time ago. You know what it was like here then?" His eyes strayed over to Lisa. "There were a couple hundred people hanging out here, coming and going, and every last one of them was on their drug of choice. It was like three years of being on another planet. Hell, I hardly remember yesterday." Henry dropped his hand from his face and looked at Will. "You missed it, didn't you? The hills were full of us. It was like an invasion, and there wasn't one single rule. We got our water from the creek, sent someone into Las Sombras every so often for food and more drugs. There were bonfires every night, and nobody could keep their clothes on, you know what I mean?" Henry nodded his head slowly. After a few seconds, he said, "What did you ask me?"

Will wondered again what he was doing here. "The girl on the bridge," he said.

"Oh yeah. It's funny someone from Guadalupe would send you here. They were up here too, you know. They might like to think they were better than us, that they didn't have any use for a bunch of long-haired hippies, but just wave a set of bare breasts in front of them and watch." He looked at Lisa. "It was the best of times," he said. "It was the worst of times."

Lisa smiled. "Sounds wild," she said.

"It was something," he said and turned to Will. "But I can't help you. It would be like trying to remember someone you met in a bar twenty-five years ago. You could ask around, though. There are still some people down below who were here back then. They've cleaned themselves up. Probably taking their kids to Little League." Henry took in a long breath of air and let it out slowly. "I never learned much history of this place, but I'll tell you, we left some of our own."

"I guess it was a foolish question," Will said.

"Yeah," Henry said. "It was a dumb thing to ask."

Lisa turned and looked at Will. "Did you hear what your friend said? Even he thinks this is stupid. And you agree with him. When I tell you that, you don't even listen."

"I'd listen to you," Henry said.

Lisa opened her mouth and then closed it. Will saw that she was smiling and biting the inside of her cheek at the same time and thought it might be time to leave before she killed the two of them.

"We better go," he said.

"You want another beer?" Henry asked.

"No thanks," Will said and stood up. The sun was down now. The air was cool and still. "We better go. When did you move up here, anyway?"

Henry watched Lisa rise and stand next to Will. "I don't know," he said. "I guess when it all turned into real estate down below. The guy who bought most of the land started selling off lots to people with money, and that kind of changed things. I managed a couple acres up here, and that was that." Henry looked past Lisa and Will, out at the valley.

"I saw something once," he said. "Nobody believed me. They said it was just the drugs in my mind I was seeing, but I swear, it happened. It was down by the creek, and I was sitting up against a cottonwood. Everything was quiet, and then all of a sudden I hear this singing. Low at first and then louder. When I looked up I saw four Mexicans dressed in those clothes they wear. You know, all in white, like peons or something, and they had these big straw hats on their heads and sandals strapped high up their ankles. Their skin was so dark it was black almost.

And they were singing and waving sticks, and all through the woods I see these pigs. Hundreds of pigs rooting around being herded by these Mexicans. I don't know where they were going. I don't know where they came from. Maybe they were spirits. But you know, I could never figure out what kind of vision this was. It was something, though."

Six

LISA DIDN'T SPEND THE night with Will, which, as things turned out, was just as well. Her mother had to be in Las Sombras early the next morning for a doctor's appointment. Since she refused to drive on highways and Mundo never got out of bed until midday, Lisa was stuck with chauffeuring.

"What kind of doctor takes patients on a Saturday morning?" Will asked.

"A bruja," Lisa said. "Herbs and powders and things. My mother doesn't go to doctors. They scare her."

They were parked off a dirt road in the woods, south of town. The light of a thin moon lay on the tops of the piñons like snow; the ground beneath was dark. A slight breeze pushed softly through the branches, moving the shadows.

"And you gave me a hard time about Henry," Will said.

They were both smoking. Lisa stretched out on the seat, her head on the armrest, her legs in Will's lap. She took a deep drag off her cigarette and exhaled slowly. Will watched the smoke drift out the window.

"Do you know the names of stars?" she asked.

"No," Will said, "I don't," and he reached inside the cuff of her pants and felt the smooth warm touch of her leg.

As soon as they had left Henry Pearson's and started back down his godawful road, Lisa had seemed to shake off the effect of the three beers she'd drunk. She sat straight up in the truck seat, a grin on her face, and leaned with the truck, smoothly into the ruts. When she glanced over at Will, her grin grew wider.

Will wasn't feeling very well. Henry's ramblings about his old hippie days had left him depressed, even if they seemed to amuse Lisa. He felt not only that he had glimpsed something slightly obscene but also that this was all a vast waste of time. Suddenly, this girl on the bridge faded away to nothing, and he couldn't understand why he'd let the whole thing take over two days of his life. It was as if he'd let some vaguely remembered nightmare from childhood have importance years later. Joe Vigil had said it earlier: "This girl has already turned to dirt."

Lisa, still grinning, said, "This Henry person seems like a very nice man. I'm sorry if I complained earlier. It's good to meet your friends, Will. Especially one who can see the spirits of pigs."

Will gave her a weak smile. "It's not quite like he's family," he said. "I'm glad you had a good time, though."

The road leveled out a bit, and Will pulled the gearshift into second.

"Are we going to visit your friends down the hill?" Lisa asked. "We could go from door to door and ask them if they remember a blond girl from the old hippie days."

"It's not pronounced 'heepie,'" Will said.

"Well, pardon me," she said. "I am bilingual, you know. Not like some people."

"That's good," Will said. "Bilingual around here means hacking apart two languages instead of one. Besides, I speak Spanish."

"So say something."

Will hit the end of Pearson's road. He turned south and hit the gas harder. "Let's get out of aquí," he said.

Lisa laughed. "Bueno," she said. "Vamanos."

Will brought Lisa home by eleven. They drove through town, which was stone dead except for the vehicles parked in front of Tito's, the only bar in Guadalupe. There wasn't much to the place. One large room with low, smoke-stained ceilings, a couple of pool tables, and a jukebox stacked with Mexican and old rock and roll tunes. There was a crowd of men off to the side of the building, drinking beer, sitting on car hoods.

"That's where my father used to live," Lisa said. "He'd come home to sleep. Sometimes."

When he got home, Will drank a slow beer sitting outside the house, up against the wall. The moon lit up the meadow and the foothills beyond. He could hear the creek, slow and steady and distant. Heat lightning flashed softly to the east, way beyond the mountains, maybe from out on the plains. Will took a last long drink of beer and put the can on the ground beside him. He thought that his life couldn't be much better than this.

They showed up when Will was asleep. Later, he guessed the scenario. They were probably some of the guys he had seen earlier outside of Tito's killing the night, or maybe inside, stalking around the pool table with a cue. When the bar closed, they bought a couple of six-packs and took a slow cruise. Maybe they parked at the river and sat in their vehicles drinking with the headlights off. Maybe they just drove up the highway and back, over and over, keeping the speed down so the Guadalupe cops wouldn't bother with them. Finally, they ended up at Will's place.

Will jerked awake, almost in a panic, as if he'd forgotten how to breathe while asleep. He could hear a parked engine screeching, revved up high. Headlights cut through the small, dusty window by his bed, igniting the entire bedroom, and he realized that whoever was outside could see him sitting up, framed in the window. They had seen him startled awake like a frightened animal. He could hear voices and then the sound of someone laughing. Something hit the roof, and by the metallic clanging as it bounced down the tin roofing, Will knew it was a beer can.

He moaned and swore softly. The voices outside grew louder. He swung out of bed and pulled on a pair of jeans. He threw on a work shirt, not bothering to button it up, and went outside barefoot.

There were two vehicles. One was a long, beat-up car sitting low to the ground. Its headlights were on high, splashing across the south side of his house like a spotlight. Will could see where the mud plaster had worn away from the wall and in some places had fallen off altogether, exposing the adobe bricks. The window frame leaned with the slope of the ground, paint flaking away from the wood. For a brief second, he was embarrassed at the sight of his house. The ground was cool beneath his feet, stones pushing up hard against the skin. He walked into the headlights. This isn't going to go smoothly, he thought.

The car engine rumbled too loudly for there to be a muffler. Behind the car, parked under a large juniper, was a small pickup that looked familiar, but it was back in the shadows and Will wasn't sure where he'd seen it before.

Two young men leaned against the car, talking low now, one of them laughing softly. Will stepped on something jagged and cursed. The voices quieted, and they watched him walk past the headlights, stopping a few feet from them. He was close enough now to see them clearly.

He knew both of them, but he didn't know from where. He'd lived long enough in Guadalupe to have seen nearly everyone, but many of the faces had no landmarks to go with them. Maybe he'd waved at them a hundred times on the road. Maybe he'd run into them at the lumberyard. He didn't know. They were both young and drunk, and Will knew they hadn't ended up at his house because of a wrong turn.

"Hey," Will said, "it's late."

Neither of them moved, and for a second Will thought that if he just backed away and went inside his house, they'd drink their beer and leave. One of them was built thick and solid, not like he'd worked at it but like he'd been born that way. He looked at Will lazily, smiling a little, and Will realized this one wasn't as drunk as he had thought. The other one was thin, a glazed look in his eyes that spread to his face and made his features look slack and empty. Will could see that he was doing all he could just to lean against the car and not fall over.

"It's not late, jodido," the heavyset one said, and he stood up straight. "It's early. You're the one who's late."

"You're an ugly fucker, you know that?" the other guy said, and the words came out of his mouth slurred.

"Eee, don't insult him. We're his guests." He reached in the side window of the car and dragged out a six-pack of beer. He pulled one loose and held the rest out to Will. "You look like you need one of these," he said.

Will stared at him until he lowered his arm. The guy looked down at the beer in his hands and shook his head slowly. "We're just trying to be friendly. You got some problem with that?" He popped open the can and took a long drink. "It tastes all right to me."

"How come you're so ugly, anyway?" his friend said. "Break him down, Lalo. I'll piss on his face."

"What do you guys want?" Will said. He didn't look at the drunk but at the one named Lalo.

"Why do you think we want anything?" Lalo said. "We came to drink a beer with you. Get to know one of you people moving in here."

Will looked back at the house. He could see the inside of his bedroom. He thought that this might go on forever and wondered if there were words to turn it another way. "I'm going back in the house," he said, turning back to Lalo. "Leave when you want to."

Lalo came a step closer, and Will could smell beer and sweat. "You think it's that easy? You think we came here by accident?" He spoke calmly, but there was a grating feel to his words, and Will could tell the guy was beginning to get into this. "How'd you get here, anyway? What sick old man did you give a few dollars to for this place? I get tired of you people coming here with your money thinking you can buy anything you want."

"Get out of here," Will said. He tried to keep his words level, but he could feel his heart speeding up, his lungs moving faster like there wasn't enough air.

"I'm not going anywhere, jodido. This is my home. Not yours." He moved closer and jabbed at Will's chest with his fist. Will stumbled back and stepped on something that cut into the sole of his foot.

"I don't even know who you guys are," Will said.

"And then I hear," Lalo went on, "that you're fucking Lisa Segura. Since she spreads her legs for everybody else in this town, I don't know why this should bother me. But it does. You're in a place you don't belong, and I'm sick of it. And now you want to stick your nose in things." Will slapped his hand away as it came at him again. "That's all I needed," Lalo said. "I'm going to knock the shit out of you."

From off to the side of them, back in the shadows by the pickup, somebody said softly, but loud enough to be heard over the car engine, "That's enough, Lalo."

Whoever it was moved away from the truck and walked toward them. He stopped next to Lalo. "Hello, Will," he said.

Will nodded. "Jimmy." Although Will didn't know him very well, they'd run into each other over the years. Will knew that he had a couple of kids and worked at the mine and that he was a friend of Mundo's. Seeing him next to Lalo, how they had the same build, Jimmy a little heavier, a little taller, and quite a bit older, Will could see the resemblance and knew they were brothers.

"I came over here to make sure they didn't mess with you," Jimmy said.

"What do you call this?" Will said.

"I call this good advice." Jimmy looked at his brother. "Isn't that what you were doing, Lalo, helping Will out?"

Lalo looked at Jimmy and spoke in Spanish. Will didn't catch it all, but enough to know that Lalo was telling

Jimmy to keep out of this. That he knew how to take care of these things.

Jimmy snorted. "Oh, sí," he said, "I saw how you take care of things." Jimmy looked back at Will. "You're still in one piece, Will. Maybe you hurt your foot." He shrugged. "That's all."

"What's going on here, Jimmy?" Will asked.

"I always thought you were good people, Will. So maybe you made a stupid mistake. That can happen. Some people get shot when they make a mistake. Others get advice. Good advice." He smiled.

"I don't understand."

"Me and Lalo's tío is Ray Pacheco," Jimmy said. "You get it now?"

Will didn't say anything for a second. He wondered just what it was that he had said to Ray that would bring his nephews to his house. "This has gotten out of hand," Will said. "I asked Ray some questions. I didn't mean to upset him."

"He's not upset, asshole," Lalo said. "We are."

"It's the truth, Jimmy," Will said. "I didn't mean for this to be a big deal."

Jimmy stared at him for a moment. Finally, he said, "That's what I thought. So go back to bed, Will. It's good we had this little talk."

Will watched them drive off, Lalo driving the car with his buddy nodding out on the seat beside him. Jimmy took his time leaving, driving slowly as if that, too, were something he wanted to say.

Will limped back into the house. He went into the bedroom, switched on the light, and looked at the clock. It was nearly four. It would be getting light in an hour. He sat down on the edge of the bed and looked at the inch-long cut on the bottom of his foot. It didn't seem to be too deep and it had bled clean. He washed it out in the bathroom, put on a pair of thick socks and went into the kitchen. He lit one of the burners on the stove and put on a pot of coffee. Smoking a cigarette, he watched the water boil up into the coffee grinds and drain back down black.

When the coffee was ready he poured a cup, grabbed a blanket off the bed and went back outside. He set up a folding chair against the side of the house and eased into it. The sky to the east was still dark, but along the rim of the mountains he could see a thin, pale line. A slight breeze carried with it the faint odor of exhaust from Lalo's car. Will covered himself with the blanket and sipped the coffee. He watched a jet blink its way slowly across the sky. He thought that people he knew had come to his house in the night and threatened him.

For him, at that moment, it was no longer about a girl on a bridge.

The first spring Will lived in Guadalupe, a storm came to the mountains, and in three days four feet of snow fell. The day before the storm, the sky had been streaked with white. It had been so warm that Will had worked outside his house in only a light shirt. By the next morning, eight inches of snow lay on the ground. The wind blew cold through the cracks in the door and around the frame of the window, and not even the mountains could be seen.

By midafternoon, twenty inches had fallen, and Will began to wonder whether the seasons in this place were going backward. Just before evening, he heard pounding on his door. When he opened it, the snow that had drifted there spilled in, and standing in the wind and dark was Telesfor Ruiz. He was dressed in overalls and a wool cap that didn't quite cover his ears. His face, which was usually gray, was a dark red. Ice was frozen in the hair beneath Telesfor's nostrils and at the corners of his mouth. The old man held a burlap bag.

It was the only time Telesfor had ever come to Will's house, and even then he merely stood for a few moments just inside the doorway. He said that the storm would be here for days and that he had brought some things for his neighbor. When Will offered to walk back with him, Telesfor said that he could walk the way blind and did not need the worry of Will becoming lost in returning.

Will watched Telesfor leave, walking slowly through snow that came far above his knees. In the burlap bag, Will found six donuts as hard as rocks, a large sack of beans, a shrunken clove of garlic, and the skinned heads of two sheep.

The sun had just cleared the mountains when Will woke. He felt hot and sweaty beneath the blanket. The metal rod of the chair was digging into his back, and he thought this was what had awakened him. Then he heard a vehicle thumping through the holes in his drive. A beat-up flatbed swung around the cottonwoods, empty drums bouncing in the back. Will threw off the blanket and sat up. He groaned, ran a hand through his hair, and then rubbed his face. The truck pulled to a stop a few yards away. The driver's door swung open, and Henry Pearson climbed out of the cab.

Either he had on the same clothes he had worn the day before or he had a supply of new blue jeans and white T-shirts a size too small. His hair was flattened down but still looked unruly, as if he'd tried to brush it and after a few swipes through had given up. His beard was as knotted and twisted as ever. He took a long look at the house and then stared down at the beer cans lying on the ground. He kicked at a can.

"You're turning into a Mexican, aren't you, Will?" he said.

"I had a tough night," Will said. "How'd you find my house?"

"I asked at the café." Henry's hand went to his face, and he began threading his fingers through his beard. "Anyway," he went on, "I'm going to Las Sombras for groceries. After you left yesterday I thought of something. Maybe you're interested?"

Will stared at him for a few seconds and then said, "Let me put on some coffee."

They brought their cups outside and sat against the side of the house in the sun. There wasn't a cloud to be seen, and whatever humidity had been in the air had already burned off.

"It's going to be hot," Henry said.

"It has been. Except for that rain the other day."

"It rains all day, and then you turn around and it's dry again. What's wrong with this country, anyway? Nothing works right."

Will looked at the ground between his legs. A black ant was tugging at something that didn't look like much to him.

Pearson took a sip of coffee. "It's nice here," he said. "Quiet. No one to mess with you."

"Once a week," Will said, "fifty people show up to play baseball just the other side of the creek."

"Where? On that field over there? Tell them to get the hell out."

"That's an idea," Will said. He pictured himself standing on the pitcher's mound telling twenty softball players, all drinking beer, to get out and take their noisy kids with them.

"All this," Henry said, waving his free hand, "used to belong to the Indians. All of it. And then the Spanish came in and butchered and stole. I've read about this stuff. That Cortéz guy, or maybe it was Onate. I forget. It doesn't matter, though. It was one of them. And now they give you this crap that they've been here forever. The land is their blood. Gringos, get the hell out, and all they really are is a bunch of thieves like everyone else."

Will wondered why Pearson lived here. He was used to hearing people bitch about everything, from their wives to the weather to how their damn truck wouldn't start. But most of them did it with some underlying sense of humor. Henry talked about things as if his life had taken a wrong turn a long time ago. Will looked sideways at him over the rim of his coffee cup. Henry was stooped down, staring straight ahead. His T-shirt stretched tight against his torso. His arms were long and bony and whiter than Will would have thought possible for early July. It made him look slightly indecent, a part of him that should have been covered.

Henry stroked his beard with his fingers. "The thing I thought about," he said, "is you might want to find out who the Guadalupe cop was back then."

Will snorted. He put his cup on the ground and stood up. The sun was climbing higher. He could smell a stale odor coming from his clothes. He needed a shower. He needed some more sleep. "I know who the cop was," he said.

"Well, he knew everything that was happening out in Canto Rodado," Henry said, looking at Will. "Everybody in Guadalupe did. This cop would come up there every few weeks and raise hell with the kids from town who were hanging out with us. Like it was okay for their niños to get drunk here in Guadalupe, but let them just think about smoking a joint with us and see what happens."

"What would he do?"

"Make noise. He'd drive up those old roads with his lights flashing and chase anybody from town back home. He left us pretty much alone, though. I'll say that much for him. But if this girl of yours was from Canto Rodado, he might know something."

"You remember any of the kids from Guadalupe?"

Pearson shrugged. "No," he said. "I didn't even know who the hell they were back then. I know this isn't much, but since I was passing by, I thought I'd tell you." He pushed himself away from the wall and stood up stiffly. "I got to go, before Las Sombras gets too hot." He walked to his truck, opened the door, and folded himself into the driver's seat. He looked at Will.

"Who was that girl you were with yesterday?" he asked.

"A friend."

"Nice friend. She doesn't have a sister, does she?"

Will didn't even try to picture Henry with a sister of Lisa's, even if she'd had one. "No," he said finally. "She's got a brother, though."

Seven

WILL STOOD UNDER THE
shower until the water ran from hot to warm to cold. He
stayed under the steady run of water and washed away
two days of sweat and dirt. His heel began to throb, and
he could see that the skin was puffed up and red around
the cut. He splashed some hydrogen peroxide on it, wondering why he hadn't done so before, then shaved in
front of the small mirror over the bathroom sink. His face
slowly became more presentable, but he could see a hag-
gard look around his eyes that the razor didn't do much
to clear up. He dressed and went into the kitchen. He
heated up a pot of beans from two days earlier and fried
a couple of eggs, putting it all together on a plate and
covering it with red chile. He got a tortilla out of the refrigerator and poured out what was left of the coffee.

He ate trying not to think. But he remembered a
winter years ago when his truck had blown a radiator hose
and left him stuck on the side of the highway about six
miles south of town. He had waited a long time in the
cold for someone to stop. When a vehicle finally pulled

up, an old pickup with a couple of guys in the cab drinking beer, the driver had leaned lazily toward him and said that if he was still there when they cruised back, they'd kill him. A wet snow was falling and it was nearly dark. Will didn't say a word. The driver smiled at him, pushed the truck into gear, and drove off. The walk back to Will's house took three hours. He remembered, even now, how he had kept his eyes down at his feet whenever he saw headlights coming at him through the snow. That was the last time Will had felt the way he did now.

He shoved his plate away and went to the open door and leaned against the frame. He stared at the empty beer cans Lalo had left lying on the ground. He knew what he was going to do. He also knew that his reasons didn't make much sense, but if he didn't think about that, then he could be truly surprised when Lisa called him stupid.

There was a lot of traffic on the road, pickups with kids and fishing poles, heading up into the mountains to fish the creeks and get away from the heat. The lot in front of the lumberyard was full. The skunks were gone from the highway, but Will could still smell them, and he could see the stains on the pavement where they'd lain.

He drove to the north end of town and pulled into the village office. It was a one-story, plastered building built years ago with state money. The mayor had a small office in the back, next to the dispatchers. The front half of the building consisted of a village council chamber, where half the town got together every month and argued, and a small visitors' area filled with maps and brochures that were faded yellow and coated with a fine layer of dust.

Monica Chavez was behind the front counter shuffling through a stack of papers. She looked up when Will came through the door. He walked up to the counter, leaned against it, and reached for a cigarette.

"No smoking," Monica said.

"I've seen the mayor in here chain-smoking," Will told her.

"So what does that have to do with you?" she asked, looking at him seriously. She cocked her head slightly. "I see your ears haven't burned to ashes." Will was nearly fifteen years older than Monica, but she treated him, as always, as though their ages were reversed. She had the same dark, quiet look in her eyes she'd had years ago when her grandfather, Marcello Rael, stooped down next to her and said, "This is the man who will build a house for you, hija."

Will had lived in his house by the creek for three years when Marcello stopped by and said that he had been thinking. Since he had long ago sold his cows and no longer needed the pasture, and since no one in his family wished to live in an old adobe that always needed repair, he thought he would like to sell the house and acreage to Will. Will, who had never owned anything of value in his life, told Marcello that he had little money and that work was sometimes hard to find. Marcello looked away and rubbed the side of his face and said again that he had been thinking. He said he would part with this land, which was so close to his heart, if Will would agree to pay him five thousand dollars cash over as much time as he needed and sign a paper promising to build a house for each of Marcello's two granddaughters. Marcello would purchase all of the building materials and Will would provide all of the labor. If Will died or left Guadalupe before the houses were built, the property would be returned to Marcello. If one of his granddaughters died, Dios perdónes, or left town, a thing even worse, a house would be built for the next granddaughter. When Will asked what if one of his granddaughters wished to have a castle built, Marcello told him not to worry, that they were reasonable men.

Marcello brought his granddaughters with him to Will's house to sign the papers, two skinny little girls all dressed up, their long black hair combed and ribboned, both of them too shy to look up from the ground. Marcello crouched down between the two of them and pointed at Will. "This is the man who will one day build a house for each of you. For your families. No, not now, Monica. When you are older." Will looked at the two girls and tried not to smile. In his soul, he thought that although Marcello was a gentle man, he was also foolish and that Will now owned a house for nothing.

Twelve years later, he and Felipe built Monica's house. Will worked weekends, nights after real work, wondering why he had been so naive as to make such a deal with a man who had so cleverly taken advantage of him. Monica and her husband and their new baby lived in a small trailer on the house site. Marcello would stop by, smoking his hand-rolled cigarettes, telling Will to make sure the corners were square, the roof watertight.

They all got drunk the afternoon the house was finished. Beer and too much tequila. Monica's sister, Estrella, was there with her boyfriend. She whispered to Will that she was engaged as though that would make him happy. Marcello stood off by himself smoking and staring at the house until the sun was gone.

Now, three years later, Will asked Monica, "Why should my ears have burned to ashes?"

"Because my roof leaks, that's why. Right on my hijo's bed. If you can make it never rain again, I wouldn't care, but I don't like it when my baby sleeps in a puddle."

"By the stovepipe, right?"

"If you know where it is," she said, "how come you can't fix it?"

"I'll come by."

Monica grunted. "Sure," she said. She leaned back in her chair, raised her eyebrows, and gently hooked a finger in her hair and moved it away from her face. "So," she said.

"How's Marcello?" Will asked.

"He's fine. Slower, but not so slow he can't go fishing." Marcello had cracked his ankle the winter before, falling on the ice outside Tito's. The fall hadn't hurt him, but the six-pack he'd been carrying had flown up in the air and landed on his ankle.

"When did you start working Saturdays?"

Monica looked down at the papers on the desk and

then back up at Will. "Since I got behind," she said. "All this has to be in the mail Monday morning."

"Ah." They looked at each other for a while, both of them smiling slightly. Finally, Will said, "Let me ask you a question, Monica. What happens to all the old village records?"

"They get stored away."

"They don't get burned after so long? Tossed out?"

Monica shrugged. "I don't know. I haven't been here that long. The records in the building go back four years."

"How about police records?"

"It's the same with them. Each month everything gets closed out and filed."

"So what if I wanted something from a long time ago?"

"Like how long?"

"Like twenty-five years long."

"Eee," she said, and leaned forward in her chair. "I don't know. There's boxes and boxes of papers in the old building out back. Maybe there. But twenty-five years ago is a long time."

Will didn't say anything. He looked at the clock on the wall behind her, the second hand creeping.

"How's Lisa?" Monica asked.

"Lisa's fine," Will said. "She's in Las Sombras with her mother."

Monica nodded and looked past Will, out the front door. There wasn't much to see. Will's truck parked next to her car. The New Mexico state flag hanging limply from the pole. The sun was reflecting off something lying on the ground in the middle of the parking lot. "You'll fix my roof so my hijo doesn't drown?"

"Oh, sí," Will said.

She reached in the desk drawer and threw a key on the counter. "There's a light switch on the wall," she said. "I don't know what is out there, but don't make a mess."

The two-room adobe sat in the weeds, looking forgotten and in utter disrepair. The roof was pitched slightly, and the multicolored roofing paper had split along the seams and was patched heavily with tar. There was a swollen look to the roof as if it were bloated with water. The glass in the one small window by the door had been broken long ago, and the plastered walls were so cracked that weeds grew from the dirt beneath. Will opened the padlock and pushed the door open. He found the light switch, and the room filled with a dim yellow light.

He could see how the vigas inside sagged from years of snowloads and how stained they were from moisture. Something fluttered against the far wall, and Will wondered whether a bird had become trapped in the room or if the building was full of bats. The entire space was jammed with junk: old push lawnmowers, a snowmobile that was half dismantled, parts kicked about the floor, a small tractor covered with dust and old oil. There were water pumps and gasoline engines that looked as if they'd been used in the last century. Rakes and shovel and picks leaned haphazardly against the walls along with coffee cans full of nails and screws and bolts. In the middle of the room was a cast-iron stove, without a stovepipe, and beside it sat a small oak table and chair. The surface of the table was thick with dust and littered with the droppings of rodents. When he stepped inside, he could smell the odor of damp and rot.

He made his way through the debris to the back room. Set in the far wall was another small window, and sunlight filtered through the cobwebbed glass. A string dangled from a lightbulb on the ceiling. It took Will a few pulls, but the bulb clicked on.

"My God," Will said softly. Boxes and boxes of paper crowded the room. They were stacked up along three walls, almost to the vigas, and layered three or four tiers deep. Some of the boxes had tipped over, and papers were spilled out on the floor. An old desk sat in the midst of all this, piled high with books, their bindings thick and warped.

Will picked up the book lying closest to him. The cover was thick and spongy and badly chewed at the corners. He could see the date, 1924, inscribed on the leather. He opened it to the middle. The date at the top of the page was June 2, and it was written awkwardly in Spanish and in large print, as if by a child. Will read slowly.

Juanito Griego, son of Juan and Estelle Griego, drowned in an irrigation ditch that runs behind

their house. Juanito's sister, Victoria, said that he
fell in and floated away too fast.

More was written below that, but it had been blurred
away by water. Will turned a few more pages.

> September 23: Tomás Rael's truck ran down the
> hill going into the village with no driver and
> killed a horse belonging to Horacio Medina.

> November 8: It snowed through the night and is
> cold. Rose García's house which sits near the
> river caught fire and burned.

> December 2: The priest of this village, Father
> Joseph, who was priest here for so long, died in
> the night.

Will placed the book back carefully and picked up another. The handwriting was the same and, again, it was
full of entries. He slid it back with the others and thought
that here, buried in this room and written in journals, was
the history of the village, at least back to 1924. He wondered who else knew of these books and why they had
been left here to decay. He felt as if he had found something of great importance that no one remembered.

Will went through all of the books. Sometimes reading, even giving the words meaning when he wasn't sure
what they meant. Sometimes he just carefully turned the
pages. The handwriting changed in 1938, but the journals

went on as if those who wrote these things slowly faded away until someone else took over. Most of the entries were still in Spanish, but a little English was mixed in. Births were noted, baptisms, deaths. The last journal was for 1945, and the last entry in it was for December 31.

> There has been no snow this winter but the air is freezing. Albert and Claudia Herrera's son, Filemon, was killed in the war. On an island in the Pacific Ocean. Father Jerome will say a mass tomorrow. Filemon was a good boy.

Will put the book back. The sunlight coming in the window had changed, and he wondered how long he had been inside. The journals were stacked neatly on the table now, and Will thought that someday he would return here and read every word written in each book.

He turned away from the desk and stared at the boxes. With a groan, he stooped down and went through the one closest to him. The outside of the box was labeled "1979, January–April." There were thick manila folders inside, one for each month. He took one out and opened it. About two-thirds of it consisted of village affairs; the rest were police reports, all in English. They were mostly about traffic violations, occasionally a fight at Tito's bar. The names were all listed, and Will noticed that Felipe was down for running over Melvin Cortéz's dog while speeding.

Will shoved the folder back in the box, thinking that this shouldn't be too hard. Delfino had given him the date, September 1968. Every carton in the row in front of him was dated in the 1970s. He took a deep breath, the smell of age and mildew, and started digging in.

When he finally found the right year, the muscles in his thighs were cramped from kneeling, and all about him was a mess of files and papers that had fallen to the floor when the damp boxes had split open. There were three cartons with the year 1968 printed on the sides. He carried them away from the debris, cupping his hands underneath so the bottoms wouldn't fall out.

The first box ran from January to April. The second one held the summer months. In the third, he found the folder for September. He laid it on the dirt floor and took out a cigarette. He crouched down, smoking and thinking that this had gone too easily. Maybe Delfino had gotten the years mixed up. Maybe it was all just talk, an old man's hallucination. Something mixed up in memories. Will brought the cigarette to his mouth and opened the file.

The first page was typed minutes from a meeting. After that were pages of forms in triplicate, applications for state funds for various projects. Will skipped through all of it and got to the police reports. The forms were standard. Name, address, time of day, who reported it, the citation issued. At the top of each paper was a line for the officer on duty to sign. On some, the name was Frank Martínez. On others, it was Ray Pacheco. The first few were traffic, one an accident south of town with no injuries. There was yet another fight at Tito's, who spent the night in jail and who was driven to the emergency room in Las Sombras for stitches.

Will found her in the back, behind everything else. The form was blank except for the name of the officer on duty, and there, printed at the top of the page and signed, was Ray Pacheco's name. Stapled to the back of the sheet of paper were two black-and-white photographs. The first one stopped Will's breath. It was a picture of a young girl, naked, hanging by the neck from Las Manos Bridge.

Donald Lucero, one of the two Guadalupe police officers, was with Monica, leaning against the counter picking at his teeth with a toothpick. Although he had been born and raised in Guadalupe, he had one of those qualities local police officers seemed to possess: no one really knew much of his life, and many were even confused as to what family he came from. It was as if Lucero had grown up in a vacuum for the sole purpose of issuing citations to his neighbors when he came of age.

He nodded as Will laid the key on the counter. "Thanks, Monica," Will said.

"I almost forgot about you," she said. "You were gone so long."

"I got lost in there."

"You straighten everything up?"

"Everything's the same disaster it was when I went in."

"I'll check, you know."

"Tell Marcello I said hello."

"Don't forget my roof."

"Never," Will said and nodded at Lucero as he turned to leave.

Will drove over to Felipe's house. There was no sign of Felipe's truck, but his kids and a couple of their cousins were outside, half naked, swinging sticks at each other and screeching. Will stuck his head out the window.

"Hey, Octaviano," he called out, "where's your dad?"

Felipe and Elena's oldest boy looked at Will and shrugged his shoulders up and down quickly. Then he swung his stick hard and caught his brother Refugio on the knuckles with a loud smack. Refugio looked as if he might faint for a second, and then he dropped his stick and fell to the ground as if he'd been shot. He writhed around in the dirt, kicking his feet and making low groaning sounds. Octaviano and the others stared at him, and then they all ran around the side of the house.

Will got out of the truck. He walked over to Refugio and helped him into a sitting position. The boy's fingers looked as short, stubby, and dirty as they always did. Will patted his back and got him to stand up. Refugio picked up his stick.

"Where's Octaviano?" he said. "I'm going to get him."

Will pointed. "That way," he said, and without a word, Refugio ran off.

Will looked at the house. Elena was standing in the open doorway. The front of her jeans was dusted with flour. She was wiping her hands together.

"He's still alive, I see," she said.

"Not without a scar."

"I'm the one with scars," Elena said. "He's already forgotten why his fingers hurt. By now, he's probably fallen on his face." As if on cue, one of the kids howled from the other side of the house. Elena smiled. "Boys," she said, "have these tiny, tiny brains."

"I was a boy once."

"Yes," she said. "And I hear you're being real smart these days."

The phone rang from inside the house. "Felipe ran down to the lumberyard," she said. "I have coffee on if you want to wait."

"No," Will said. "Go get the phone. I'll run over there."

The lumberyard was open only until noon on Saturdays. When Will pulled up in front, it was a good thirty minutes past that. Felipe's truck was parked beside Joe's and Lawrence's. The door was locked, but when Will cupped his hands and peered through the glass, he could see Lawrence inside staring back at him. He was smiling, and he pointed at his wrist and mouthed, "Closed."

"C'mon," Will yelled. "I'm looking for Felipe."

Lawrence got off his stool, wearing a pained expression now. He unlocked the door and pushed it open. "Twelve o'clock, the sign says."

"I know," Will said. "How come you're here? I thought you were always the first one out."

"Funny."

Will moved out of the sun into the store. "Damn," he said, "it's hot. Where's Felipe?"

"He's in the office with Joe."

Joe was behind his desk, stretched out in his chair, his hands behind his head. He looked half asleep. Felipe was sitting on one corner of the desk, his arms folded, a Styrofoam cup in his hand. Will took the step up into the office.

"Late, as usual," Joe said. "If we're closed, Will comes by."

"You ought to park in the back if you don't want company," Will said. "What happened to the skunks?"

Joe shrugged. "We got a complaint."

"Imagine that." Will looked at Felipe. "What's wrong?" he asked.

"Nothing's wrong," Felipe said, which was not the truth. For the second day in a row, Felipe found himself in a lousy mood. He'd had an argument with Elena that morning, while still in bed, about how his junk pile, which only grew bigger and was full of used building materials and odd pieces of metal that Felipe found interesting, was beginning to irritate her again. "You'll feel bad," Elena had said, "when Octaviano falls into the pile and cuts his head off." Later, after a meager breakfast, when he went outside to put some order to these things,

Felipe had found himself surrounded by his children and their cousins, who were all waving sticks and hitting each other and running around without clothes. He thought that of all the children he knew, his were the only ones who were deaf when their father spoke.

Felipe had fled his house to have a quiet cup of coffee with Joe. Now, seeing Will, the day before came back to him and how Will had dragged him to see Delfino about a girl who wasn't even smart enough to hang herself where she wouldn't bother people. He thought maybe an argument would cheer him up. "Nothing's wrong," he said again. "I just get tired of doing your work."

"What work?" Will asked.

"Getting the redwood ready for Monday."

"I already did that."

"Now you tell me. After I waste half my day."

"So quit wasting time," Will said, "and go back home."

"Eee," Joe said, slapping his hand on the desk. "I don't believe you two. People let you on job sites?"

"Don't look at me," Will said. "It's Felipe. If you say it's dark, he talks about how bright the moon is. If you say it's hot, he puts on a coat."

Lawrence called out from the front that he was leaving and would lock the door after him. Joe yelled back that he'd come by Lawrence's house in a little while.

"We're going for wood," Joe told Will.

"You're going for wood already? It's only July."

"It's July now," Joe said.

People from Guadalupe seemed to start hauling wood as soon as they were done burning it. Will would see pickups winding up into the foothills as early as May and returning late in the day with loads of piñon and spruce stacked above the cab. It always depressed him, not only because his own woodpile looked like nothing but scattered bark but also because it made it seem to him that summer was just a brief pause before winter fell over the village once again.

"Will waits for December to get wood," Felipe said. "And when he runs out in January, he comes and steals mine."

Will looked at Felipe. Although the expression on Felipe's face was serious, Will could tell he was having a good time. "You told me you had plenty," Will said, "and to take what I needed. And it wasn't January, either." He reached in his back pocket. "I found something," he said.

Will laid the photographs in the center of the desk. Joe leaned forward for a better look. He breathed out a long, slow whistle. "Jesus," he said softly. Felipe didn't move. He didn't know what he was seeing at first, and when it became clear that Will had just placed before him two pictures of the girl on the bridge, he shut his eyes. Somehow Will had opened a door that should have remained closed, and Felipe knew no good would come of this.

She looked far more naked on the desk than she had when Will opened the file. She looked like she wanted to move her hands and cover herself, turn her face away from their eyes. The photos were black and white, and everything looked gray. The sky, the water, the hills, the girl's skin. One photo was of her hanging from the bridge. Her limbs were slack and her legs were slightly apart. Her toes were pointed down like a dancer's and her shoulders were slumped. She was staring at the camera, but the picture had been taken from a distance and it was difficult to make out her features. Felipe could tell her hair was light. He could see the dark line of the rope around her neck and how it rose behind her and wrapped around one of the trestles. He could see the cows on the far bank of the river.

The other photograph was up close, after she'd been taken down. Someone had straddled her body and aimed the camera down. Will could see the slats of the bridge beneath her and a grayness between them that was water. The picture caught her from just below the waist and up. Her head was turned slightly to the side. Her eyes were open, and Will thought that maybe they were actually glazed or something, but the angle of her head and the half-lidded look of her eyes gave her a dreamy expression. Her hair was short and in disarray, but he could make out the part on her scalp and could tell she would brush her hair to the side. Her mouth was full and parted, and he could see the even line of her teeth. There wasn't a mark on her body. She seemed flawless, from the curve of her shoulders to the fullness of her breasts to the flatness of her belly.

The three of them stood around the desk and stared at her. "Jesus," Joe said again. "Damn, Will, where'd you get these?"

"They were stored away in the back of the old village office," Will said. "Do you know what's in that building? There are journals that go back seventy years. Entries written down for each day. Who was born. Who died. How much it snowed. You wouldn't believe what I read in there."

What Felipe couldn't believe was that his friend, whose brain seemed to have left town, was babbling about old books while sitting before him were pictures of a dead girl that Will should never have taken from his pocket. He looked up at Will. "You broke into the village office?" he asked.

"I got the key from Monica."

"Monica gave you the key," Felipe repeated. He blew some air out of his mouth and shook his head and looked down at the floor.

"There was a report filed along with the pictures," Will said. "Ray's name was at the top."

"What did it say?" Joe asked.

"Nothing. No name. No date. Just these pictures and Ray's signature."

Felipe looked at the photographs again. He thought that Delfino had been right. This girl didn't look dead. She looked like she was resting, like when she woke she would be full of life. He also thought it wasn't right for him to be looking at her this way. He reached out and turned the pictures face down. "I don't believe you have these," he said.

"What do you mean?"

"I mean, I don't believe you have these." He looked

at Will. "What are you going to do with them? Put them up around town? Keep them in your wallet?"

"I don't know what I'm going to do with them," Will said, and he flipped the photographs back over. "But look at her. There's not a mark on this girl. Something's wrong with all this."

Will left the store with Felipe trailing a few steps behind. Joe was still inside. He had called Lawrence before they left and told him to forget about going for wood, that he was going to buy some beer and go home and sit beneath his apple tree and get a little drunk. Felipe walked Will to his truck. They both leaned against the hood.

"I don't remember it ever being this hot," Felipe said. He wiped at his forehead and his hand came away damp. "Jimmy came by yesterday," he went on. "He wanted to know what you were thinking. He said you were messing with his family and you should know better." Felipe turned his head and looked at Will. "You know Ray is his uncle?"

"I know that now," Will said. "Jimmy and Lalo came by the house last night."

"I don't know what you're doing," Felipe said, "but if you don't stop soon, this could get crazy."

Will looked at him for a few seconds and then shook his head. "I'm getting all confused in this, Felipe. I got home last night and this girl was out of my head like smoke. And then Jimmy and Lalo show up and treat me like some stupid gringo and I get pissed off and end up at the village office. Now we got these photographs and I'm wondering again who this girl is and how did she end up on a bridge in nowhere."

Felipe stared at Will. He thought there were a number of things he could say about Will being a stupid gringo, but he let it go. What he did say was, "What do you mean, 'we got these photographs'?"

Will smiled. "Did I say that?"

"Yes, you said that," Felipe said. "We don't have these pictures, you do, and whatever you do, you better be careful."

"You think this is nuts, don't you?"

Felipe pushed away from the truck. "Don't ask me," he said. "If I think too much about this, I'll be as confused as you are."

Eight

WILL STOPPED AT TITO'S to pick up a pack of cigarettes and a six-pack of beer. Fred Sánchez was drinking alone in the bar, and he held Will up for a few minutes asking about work. When Will told him work was slow and that he'd call if things picked up, Fred nodded, his glass to his lips, and stared vacantly away. "Bueno," he said.

When he got home, Will popped open a beer and lit a cigarette. He sat in the shade of the open doorway and watched a flock of small birds suddenly pick up and fly from one side of a hill to the other, disappearing up a canyon. He looked for what might have startled them and saw nothing. The empty beer cans still lay on the ground, and Will thought that he should pick them up. Instead, he finished his beer and went indoors.

He wandered around the inside of his house for a while, then rinsed out the coffee cups he and Henry had used that morning. Then he went to the place in the wall where the Lady stood. He moved the calendar from the opening, took the two pictures from his pocket, and put them there. He thought that he now had two women hidden in his wall, and he understood neither of them.

Will went into his bedroom, lay down on the bed, and pushed open the window. He stared outside for a while at his truck parked in the driveway, then rolled over and gazed up at the ceiling. There were four vigas above his bed. The bark had been removed with a drawknife, leaving deep gouges in the wood, and the limbs had been snapped off with the butt end of an ax. There was a dark stain on one of the vigas where it butted into the wall, and for the first time Will thought that it wasn't grease or pitch or mud, but blood.

Just before sleep, he remembered the day Telesfor Ruiz had told him that his father had died in the mountains when Telesfor was grown and with his own family, and that he had not been with his father when he died. A thing, he said, he often thought of even now.

Telesfor's father, who was born Eloy Ruiz and who cut firewood and latillas and vigas for the people of Guadalupe, did not return home one day. That night his wife, Berna, walked to Telesfor's house and told him she knew in her heart that his father was dead and by himself. Telesfor had gone into the mountains to where his father had cut for years and had found him as his mother had said. Telesfor's father was beneath a spruce tree that had fallen across both his legs. He was sitting upright, and his upper body lay across the trunk of this tree as if embracing it.

After the burial, Berna Ruiz asked Telesfor to go into the mountains and bring back the tree that had killed her husband. He brought to his mother's house each piece of wood, each limb and branch from the tree. He stacked it beside the large woodpile his father had gathered over the years, and there it sat, untouched and unburned forever. Each morning until her own death, Telesfor's mother would walk outside and stand before it and say nothing out loud, as if she and this tree knew something no one else did.

When Will awoke, he was facing the window, and the first thing he saw was Lisa's car parked beside his truck. The sun had set. The air coming in the window was both cool and warm. He could hear movement in the kitchen and then footsteps coming through the house into the bedroom. The bed shifted as she sat beside him.

Lisa put her hand on the back of his neck and threaded her fingers along his scalp. "I know you're awake," she said.

Will groaned. She balled up her hand and gave his hair a slight tug. "I go to Las Sombras," she said, "and I come back and find you still in bed."

Will grunted and rolled over. "How long have you been here?"

"I drank a beer outside," she said. "I watched the sun go down. I waited for you to wake up."

"Is your mother here?"

"No," Lisa said. "I took my mother home." The shadows were growing in the room and shaded parts of her face, making her eyes look darker, deeper than they were. She smiled. "You did nothing today?"

"I did a few things."

"Hmm." She reached behind her neck and undid the clasp holding her hair. She shook her head gently and her hair fell about her face, dropping below her shoulders. "I have a few things for you to do," she said, and she tugged her blouse loose from her jeans.

They were sitting at the kitchen table. Dinner hadn't been much, a couple of cheese sandwiches with green chile, but Will had made a pot of strong coffee and it tasted fine. He lit a cigarette. Lisa reached for the pack and took one out for herself. The kitchen door was wide open, and Will watched the draft take the smoke out of the house.

Lisa was stretched in her chair facing the open doorway, her legs out before her, her bare feet crossed at the ankles. She took a deep drag off the cigarette and exhaled slowly. "This is my first one today," she said. "If I smoke around my mother, she tries to slap me."

"I want to ask you a question," Will said.

"Yes?"

"This is only a question. Don't look for more in it, because it's not there. All right?"

Lisa's eyes moved from the doorway to Will. "Is this a trick question?"

"No," Will said. "It's probably a stupid question, but there's no trick."

"So ask."

"Someone mentioned to me that you've slept with everyone in Guadalupe."

Lisa stared at him for a moment. She brought her cigarette to her mouth and blew the smoke out slowly. She looked back out the open door. "Is this your question?"

"Yes."

She nodded. "And I shouldn't get angry or scream at you for not minding your own business because it's only a question."

"That's right," Will said.

Lisa smoked quietly for a few seconds. "If I asked you this question, what would you say?"

"I'd answer it."

"Yes, but you would treat it like a joke. It would make you feel proud to have this question asked. That if it was true it would make you a better hunter or something. Not a whore."

Will didn't say anything for a while. Finally, he said, "You're right. If I didn't say that, I'd feel it. I won't ask you this. Forget it."

She looked at him and smiled. "Sure," she said, "forget it." She took a last hit off her cigarette and threw the butt overhand out the door. She leaned back in her chair. "For a long time," she said, "if I didn't like someone, I would sleep with him." She shrugged her shoulders slightly. "Who knows why? But I found out there are a great number of men in this village that I don't like. Does that answer your question? I'm not ugly, and at the café I knew many of them came because of me. We would drive and drink some beer and then park somewhere, and the next night it would be someone else."

Will put his cigarette out in the ashtray. He thought that there were some things better not asked.

"What you heard is true," Lisa said, "although I don't think I made it through the whole village."

"How did Mundo feel about this?"

Lisa turned her head and looked at him. "Joaquín? He hated it. We'd fight and I'd tell him to watch out for his own life and to keep out of mine. There are some things you don't understand between me and my brother, Will. I know how he seems to you, but when we were small my father would come home drunk all the time. He would beat up on Joaquín. He would beat up on my mother. But it was Joaquín who always got it the worst. My father never touched me because my brother would hide me in the back of the closet when he saw my father coming. This went on for years. Until our father died."

Will looked out the open door. He couldn't see anything past the small rectangle of light. When he turned back to Lisa, he asked, "Did you go out with me because you disliked me?"

She stared at him for a long time and then smiled. She rose from her chair and stood straight and stretched her arms over her head, her blouse pulling up until Will could see skin. She moved her chair to the table and sat across from him.

"No," she said. "I didn't know you enough to not like you. I went with you because I was so cold in that storm and you had the heater on." She leaned against the table and rubbed her mouth back and forth against Will's, her eyes open. He felt her lips tighten as she smiled. "Who's gossiping about me?" she asked, and he could taste chile and smoke on her breath.

"Sounds like it could be just about anyone," he said.

She grinned. "You taste like coffee," she said, and she brought her mouth down hard on his. Then she sat back in her chair. "A nice little talk," she said.

"It was Lalo Pacheco," Will said. "He and a friend of his and his brother Jimmy came by last night to tell me to stop bothering their Tío Ray. Your name came up."

"I hope you defended me."

"I was more concerned with surviving."

"They really came here and did that?"

Will nodded. "Jimmy said he came along to keep the peace. Lalo pushed me around and called me names."

Lisa smiled. "Poor baby," she said. "I'll have Joaquín shoot them for us."

"Good. Would he do that for me?"

"No, but he would for me." She stared at him for a moment and then leaned across the table. "I told you," she said, and for the first time Will could hear anger in her voice. "You don't listen to me. You don't listen to anybody. I hope you told them you were crazy for a day and that you came to your senses."

"Came to my senses?"

"Don't make fun of me."

Will picked up his coffee. It had grown cold. He drank it down anyway. "I told them that I didn't mean to upset their uncle and it wasn't a big deal."

"And then what?"

"What do you mean, 'And then what?'"

"I know you well enough to know that there's always more," she said.

They stared at each other until finally, Will said, "They said the wrong things, Lisa. I never messed with Ray. I asked him some things. I wasn't rude, and I left when he wanted me to. Suddenly, I've got his whole family over here. So this morning I took a drive and found some pictures of the girl."

Lisa didn't say a word for a few seconds. Then she said, "You have pictures? Where did you get these pictures?"

"Well," Will said.

Lisa shook her head. "I don't think I want to hear any more about this," she said. "I don't want to hear about this girl. I don't want to hear about Lalo and Jimmy. I especially don't want to hear about what you think. I would like you much better, Will, if you never opened your mouth again."

Nine

WILL LEFT LISA ASLEEP in bed. She was curled up under the sheets with only the top of her head visible. He stood beside the bed for a moment and listened to her breath, a soft sound coming from her mouth when she exhaled. She was resting easy now, but at night sometimes she would move around the bed as if being chased. Other times, he'd wake with different parts of her strewn across his body, or she'd be fetaled up where the wall met the bed, so far away from him it was as if he were sleeping alone. He watched her for a little while longer and then went quietly out of the bedroom.

In the kitchen, he put on a pot of coffee and then opened the front door. Not a breath of air. The sky was a cloudless blue. A day to do anything, Will thought.

By the time Lisa woke up, he had managed to pick up the empty beer cans and rake up some of the debris around his woodpile. He had cleaned up the kitchen and was drinking a second cup of coffee when Lisa walked into the room. She brushed her hair from her face. "Where's breakfast?" she asked.

Will cooked while Lisa sat outside in the sun drinking coffee. He scrambled half a dozen eggs, threw in the left-over chile from the night before, and heated up a couple of tortillas. He took the plates and the coffeepot outside, and they ate without saying much.

Will got two fishing poles out of the shed behind his house and dug up some worms from the soft dirt along the creek. They walked the stream, fishing the holes without any luck. Will thought maybe he and Lisa were making too much noise or maybe the day was just too warm and the fish were too lazy to give a damn about eating. They walked east for more than a mile, around the base of the foothill and far up the canyon. The brush became thicker and the creek narrowed, running faster over fallen trees and around boulders. The holes were harder to spot, and they had to scramble to get to them, constantly snagging their lines. Lisa hooked a couple of small trout. She unhooked them gently and held them close to her face, looking at them as if they were a disgrace because they were so small. She tossed them both back and watched them sit stunned in the water until they finally darted off, disappearing into some dark hole.

Sometime after noon, they started back down, fishing the same holes they'd hit earlier. But it was hot now, even in the shade, and Will could feel the sweat sticking to his body. He gave up after a while and watched Lisa. She would stoop down near the water and toss the bait into the creek through the brush and tight limbs of juniper. Nothing was hitting, but it wasn't so bad, Will thought, just to sit and watch her. She told him she could actually see the fish put their tail ends to the worm and swim away as if they were smarter than she. "I hate fish like that," she said.

They got back to the house by midafternoon and drank a beer inside where it was cool. When Will suggested a nap, Lisa smiled and said she needed to run home for a little while, but if he made dinner, maybe, if she wasn't doing anything else, she'd come back.

He drove down to the Guadalupe market and picked up two pounds of ground beef, a dozen hamburger buns, and all the relishes he could think of. He bought some ice cream, whipped cream, and strawberries that looked as if they'd been sitting in the cooler for too long. He had flour and eggs at home and thought that it couldn't be too difficult to bake some kind of cake. He was standing in the check-out line thinking about what a woman would do after being fed such a meal when the girl at the register, the owner's granddaughter, who must have been all of twelve, told him in a sour tone that he owed her twenty dollars and change. He paid her and left.

When Will got back to his house, Ray Pacheco's blue pickup was parked in the drive. Will could see that Ray was sitting alone in the front seat. He pulled up next to Ray and climbed out of the truck with his groceries. Will looked at him over the hood of his truck and nodded. "Ray," he said.

Ray gave him a blank stare and said, "Let's take a

drive." Even on such a warm day, Ray was wearing a light coat with the collar turned up at his neck. He had on the same cap he'd been wearing a few days before. It was cocked back, revealing a line of pale skin on his forehead.

"A drive where?" Will asked.

Ray didn't answer. After a few seconds, Will said, "Let me put these bags inside." Then he turned and went into the house. He put the things away slowly, glancing out the door every so often. Ray was still sitting motionless in the cab of his truck, staring straight ahead, one arm hanging out the open window. He thought it was probably good that Ray had come here, that maybe they could fix this misunderstanding without threats or insults. Will closed the door to the refrigerator and leaned against it. He could feel his heart beating a little too fast. About the last thing he wanted to do was climb into Ray's truck and take a ride.

Will went back outside. He walked up to the truck and asked Ray if he wanted to get out. They could drink a beer.

"Get in," Ray said, and for no reason at all, Will did.

They headed out his drive, taking the road as it circled around the baseball field, which looked empty and overgrown, as if no one ever used it, beer and pop cans lying around. A mile later they hit the highway. Ray turned east toward town. He picked up a pint bottle on the seat between them and held it out to Will. It was half empty.

"No thanks," Will said. Ray's face looked puffed up and heavier than it had a few days ago, the skin dragging down at his eyes. He didn't look as if he'd slept much. If he had, it hadn't come easy.

Ray screwed the lid off the bottle and took a drink. He put the bottle back on the seat, close to his leg. A couple of vehicles passed them coming the other direction. Ray took his hand from the steering wheel and waved. They drove by Felipe's truck in the middle of town, all three of his kids with him in the cab. Felipe threw up a hand at Ray and then did a double take when he saw Will.

Ray took the highway north for a quarter mile and pulled into the Guadalupe gas station. He stopped the truck away from the pumps, got out, and went inside, a slight hitch in his walk, his hands in the pockets of his coat. Will watched him dig out his wallet and give Norman Ortiz, the owner, some money. Neither of them said much. They shook hands and nodded, Norman saying loudly enough that Will could hear, "Bueno, Ray. We're even." Ray walked out of the station and climbed back into the truck. He took another drink from the pint, put the truck in gear, and drove off again.

About a mile out of town, Ray swung the truck wide onto the shoulder and turned, heading back the way they had come.

"You started a big mess," Ray said, his eyes straight ahead.

Will reached for the bottle on the seat and unscrewed the cap. It was cheap bourbon, which didn't matter much to Will one way or the other. He took half a swallow and felt it burn the back of his mouth, corroding its way down his throat. He looked out the side window at an adobe house whose yard was full of chickens, the ground pecked bare. An old woman wearing a faded pink dress and heavy boots stood in the shade under her portal. She watched them drive by and gave a wave.

Ray moved his eyes toward Will. Will could see a tint of yellow around the pupil. "I hear you got pictures. Out of the old village office. You're showing them around. Why are you pushing this? That's what I want to know." He put out his hand for the bottle, and Will gave it to him.

They were back in the center of town, driving slowly, the vehicles behind them passing, each driver flicking up a hand as they went by. It was late Sunday afternoon and hot. Felix's Café was quiet, the front door propped open. Will couldn't see in the windows, but he could picture Felix García inside sitting mute in the shadows by the jukebox. Tito's was a little livelier. There was a group of young guys outside drinking beer on the shaded side of the building. Will didn't see Jimmy or Lalo or anyone else he knew. The lumberyard was dead to the world, the smell of skunk finally gone, burned out of the air by the sun. The bourbon sat heavy in Will's stomach.

"I'm not pushing this, Ray," he said.

Ray glanced over at him. "What do you call it?"

"I don't know what I call it," Will said. "This was a story I wanted to know. That's the reason I went to your house. I wanted to hear more of it. Then all of a sudden, it turned into a big deal. Your nephews come over and threaten me. Push me around. And that's when I got the pictures." Will ran a hand through his hair. "I don't understand any of this, Ray," he said. "I swear I don't." He dropped his arm to his lap and looked out the windshield, thinking that although what he'd said was true, somehow the words sounded empty, even to himself. And for the first time he realized that not only had this girl been dead for years upon years, but she had no place here. He saw himself in this village asking questions about something no one wanted to talk about or even cared about. He had used Monica and had rummaged through the old village office, and then he had gone to the lumberyard with pictures of this girl as if they were a treasure he had found.

"Maybe I made a mistake," Will said.

"Maybe you did," Ray said. "You should have thought about that before." And just like that, Will felt himself grow angry. He smiled a little and thought that in the cab of this truck, there were no words either one of them could say to make things clear.

Ray turned his head and pointed with his chin past Will out the side window. "That's where she's buried," he said.

The Guadalupe cemetery sat up on a hill and was fenced in with old cedar posts and sagging barbed wire that was twisted with weeds. It was full of wood crosses that someone always seemed to keep painting white, and planted in the ground everywhere were plastic flowers so bright that the cemetery seemed like a child's drawing.

"She's buried in the northwest corner," Ray went on. "Up against the fence. Me, Frank Martínez, he's dead now, and the backhoe operator, Simon Chacón, buried her. I had to talk the priest, back then it was Father

Leonardo, into letting us bury her there. He didn't feel it was right. I told him that maybe the girl was Catholic, and besides, there was nowhere else. He even said some words over her."

A narrow road led up the hill to the cemetery. Will couldn't see much of it from the highway. A few crosses, some splashes of color. He thought for this girl to be buried there seemed as out of place as she'd been hanging from Las Manos Bridge.

"What was her name?"

Ray opened his mouth and then closed it. After a few seconds, he said, "I don't know. I never knew her name. I just buried her, and I made sure the priest came."

"You didn't report any of this to the county or the state or whoever you were supposed to notify, did you?"

"Why do you think that?"

"I saw the pictures. She didn't look like someone who'd hung herself."

Ray kept driving. Past the bridge south of town where the creek crossed the highway, they climbed the grade where the road twisted into the foothills and left Guadalupe behind.

"I should have burned those damn pictures," Ray said. "I was a police officer for thirty years. I kept half this village out of trouble. Do you hear me? I don't have nothing to explain to someone like you. Or anyone else."

They went on for a couple more miles. The road flattened out and was hemmed in on both sides by tall piñon. Ray swung off the highway and aimed the truck back toward Guadalupe. Will wondered if they were going to drive back and forth forever. This drive with Ray and the conversation were going in the same direction. Nowhere.

"I got cancer inside me," Ray said. "It's in my bowels. I don't eat so much no more. It's hard to take a crap. They say they can cut and rewire me so I can shit in a bag. I told them no." Ray turned his face toward Will, and maybe for the first time they took a good look at each other. "My wife knows this," he went on, "and now you." He looked back at the highway. "I hoped Jimmy could have talked some sense into your head. You been here a long time now, and I thought you'd see what you were risking. But I was wrong." He went a little heavier on the gas. "You're just another outsider who comes here and thinks he knows everything."

They went back through town, driving faster now. Ray didn't even bother to return the waves coming from the other vehicles. He drove by the turn that would have taken them to Will's house. Will thought of Lisa. He thought about strawberries and whipped cream and a cake he wasn't going to make and then wondered why the thought had even crossed his mind.

Two miles north of town, Ray pulled off the highway and cut west on a dirt road. He put the truck in second gear, glanced at Will, and reached again for the bottle. He took a long swallow, cutting the alcohol level down to the dregs.

"Where are we going?" Will asked. "I need to be somewhere soon."

"You'll see," Ray said, and he dropped his hand to just below his belt. Will watched his fingers push in and out on his stomach, massaging.

It was a slow, five-mile ride to the river. The road was hard-packed adobe and rutted out badly in places where somebody had tried to drive it wet. Ray swung the truck off the road and up on the side when the ruts got too deep, driving over sagebrush.

"The doctor told me maybe a year, but maybe not that long," Ray said. The ruts pulled at the wheels. Ray jerked the steering wheel to the right and leveled out the truck. "They could give me pills if the pain gets too bad. I could check into the VA hospital in Albuquerque. That's what the rest of my life is going to be."

Will stared ahead out the windshield. He could see the dark rim of the gorge now. "What are we doing out here, Ray?"

Ray picked up the pint and drained it, then tossed the bottle out the open window. His fingers went back to his stomach. The truck limped along in first gear, and the breeze coming into the cab brought dust along with it.

"I did what was right with that girl," he said. "Me and Frank took her down from that bridge and gave her a decent burial." He leaned his body a bit toward Will. "She was dead already. You hear what I'm saying? You think I could breathe life into this girl again?"

"What about her family?"

"If she cared about her family, she wouldn't have been here."

Will turned and looked at Ray. "That's a thing to

say," he said. "What about the ones who put her up there?"

"I don't know who put her up there," Ray said.

"That's what happened though. Isn't it?"

Ray was quiet for a moment, and then he said, "It don't matter no more."

They came to the edge of the gorge, and Ray turned off the truck. The gorge was far too deep to see the river, and stretching away from them in all directions was just the flatness of the valley. Will could see the vertical rock walls opposite them where the earth had split to cradle the river. Swallows darted out of the shadows. A hawk glided far to the west with its wings outstretched. The wind was blowing harder out here. Will could hear it through the sagebrush, that and the ticking of the engine.

"This was good country once," Ray said. "It never gave you much, but it never took nothing away from you neither." He pushed open the door and climbed out. The wind grabbed at his hat and he pulled it down low on his forehead. "Venga," he said.

Will got out of the truck and followed Ray to the rim of the gorge. Will could see the river snaking itself along hundreds of feet below him, the water brown and murky, the level low now because most of the snowmelt was over. The gorge cut through the earth north and south as far as he could see.

"My father kept sheep on the other side," Ray said. "When I was a boy, my brother and me would spend summers out here. We'd go back to Guadalupe in October for school. We kept the coyotes away from the lambs.

Four hundred sheep we had, and I never forgot what it was like to wake up early in the morning and see them scattered out through this valley. We'd lamb them in March, and in April, before the river got too high, we'd help our father bring them here to graze. I wouldn't see my father for two months, and then he'd come to the village when school was out and bring us back out here with him. My mother would come out every two weeks or so and bring us food and sweet candies and whiskey for my father." He turned and looked at Will. "That's the way it used to be."

Will looked across the river. The sun was arching down now, the sky hazy with dust. The color of the sage and the thin grass was a pale green. Ray moved away from him a few yards. He bent over and picked something up.

"Obsidian," Ray said. "For arrowheads." He stood up and turned around so that he was facing Will. He made a grunting noise, then put his hand in his coat pocket and took out a revolver. It was big in his hand and shone dully as though it had just been oiled. It's his police revolver, Will thought. He's still got it after all these years. Ray tapped the gun gently against his thigh and looked down at it as if he were embarrassed that Will had seen it. "I forget your name," Ray said.

Will felt his mouth open and close, and then he didn't bother with it. Something gave way in the joints of his knees, and he took a small step to balance himself. The wind gusted and took off Ray's hat. It danced away, finally snagging in the sage. Ray's hair was flattened with crease lines where his hat had pressed against his scalp. He took a deep breath and exhaled slowly. "You should have listened," he said. "I guess we both made a big mistake."

Ray raised the gun until it was level with Will's face. He crossed himself with his free hand and said softly, "Vaya con Dios." Then he jerked his arm up as if it were tied to a string, put the muzzle under his chin, and pulled the trigger.

Ten

WILL WATCHED RAY FALL.
He went down without making a sound. The wind blew
the noise of the shot at Will, and that's all he heard. Like
thunder, it seemed to him, dull and rolling. The sound
was almost a place in itself, and some part of Will knew
that he didn't want to be around when it ended.

He didn't know how long he stood there staring.
Until he could hear the wind again in the sage. Until he
heard a long, slow whisper of a sigh come out of Ray's
body. Will heard himself say something he didn't understand. He could see Ray's face. He could see the mess the
top of his head had become, the blood in the dirt pool-
ing down to his shoulders. The only thing Will was
conscious of at that moment was the desire not to get one
step closer to Ray. He looked past where Ray had fallen
and saw the hat still snagged in the sagebrush. It moved
when the wind hit it, but still it was stuck.

Will turned around and walked away. His legs felt
weak and his hands were shaking badly. He walked maybe
a hundred yards and then circled around, stumbling his

way through the brush to Ray's truck. He leaned against the hood and tried to catch his breath, the air wheezing in and out of his lungs. He tried to think about what he should do. An anxiousness grabbed hold of him, and he began to tremble again. He had the truck door open and was climbing inside the cab when he cursed loudly and got back out and walked over to where Ray lay. He knelt beside the body, one knee soaking up blood, and put his hand where he thought he might find a pulse. He pressed his palm into the flesh on the side of Ray's throat for a long while and then slid his hand inside Ray's shirt and held it there against his chest. He gave it some time to be sure. And then he went back to the truck and got the hell out of there.

Will drove too fast, hitting the potholes and small arroyos that knocked him around the cab and bounced the truck chassis hard on the springs. Finally, he swung the truck off the road and just drove over the sagebrush, swerving once to avoid the whiskey bottle Ray had thrown out not so long ago. After a few miles, he felt himself leveling off, not quite so shaky, his breath easing in and out more calmly. Will realized that he was going back to Guadalupe in Ray's truck, and he had a feeling this wasn't going to look so good.

He hit the highway and felt the shakes coming back. He lit a cigarette, hoping it would have a soothing effect. But the muscles were dancing in his thighs and his heart was speeding up, tripping in his chest as though it had lost all sense of timing. A couple of vehicles passed by him, the drivers waving and then glancing back sharply as if they hadn't seen right. Will pulled the sun visor down and drove to the village office.

The place was closed up and empty. There wasn't a vehicle parked in the lot. No sign of Donald Lucero's squad car. Will didn't even bother to get out of the truck. He circled the parking lot, got back on the highway, and drove to Felipe's. He didn't have any better luck there, which, he thought, was probably just as well; Felipe and his family didn't need any of this in their lives. But Will cursed him just the same. For fishing, for being with his kids, for having dinner with his relatives instead of being home to help him out. It crossed Will's mind that he could just drive the truck back to Ray's house. He could tell Ray's wife that Ray was at the river and needed a ride back, tell her she might want to bring someone with her. Instead, he went home. He drove through Guadalupe feeling like a neon sign, waving back at everyone who flicked up a hand at him.

Lisa's car was parked outside his house. A small fire was burning in the firepit. Lisa's making dinner, he thought. She came out of the house when he drove up and stood in the doorway. She wiped her hands down on her jeans. She was smiling.

"I thought you were going to cook," she said. Will shut off the engine and climbed out of the cab. He leaned against the pickup and tried to smile. Lisa glanced at Ray's truck and then brought her eyes back to him. She must have seen something in his face because her expression went slack and she said, "What happened?"

Lisa made the call. Will sat at the kitchen table. Every so often he could feel a splash of heat shoot through his body like a fever. Lisa called the Guadalupe dispatcher number, and a machine gave her another number to call. When she finally got someone on the line, she said that she wanted to report a death and that Donald Lucero should come to Will Sawyer's house by the baseball field. She started to give directions but then cut it short and said it was the land Marcello Rael owned with the old house on it. She said yes a few more times, ended with, "Bueno," and put the phone down. Her back was to Will. She lowered her head and brought her hands up to her face.

"Lisa," Will said.

Lisa took her hands from her face, shook her head slightly, and let out a long breath of air. "What are you going to do now?" she asked without turning around.

"I'll wait for Lucero," Will said, "and tell him what happened." She spun around and faced him. "No, you stupid, I mean after that."

"What do you mean, where am I going to go? I'm not going anywhere. The man shot himself, Lisa."

"He shot himself?" She was yelling now, leaning across the table. "You killed him, Will. You think everyone won't know that? What are you, anyway? Crazy? This stupid? If I want to kill you for this, how do you think his family will feel?" She let out a long, low moan that rose higher in pitch. She picked up the ashtray on the table and flung it at Will. It hit him full in the mouth and fell back on the table, spinning until it lay still. Will felt a

trickle of blood down his chin. Lisa let out another howl
and pounded the tabletop with the flat of her hands. She
picked the table a few inches off the floor and slammed it
back down, and then, without a word or even a look, she
turned and went out the door. Will heard her car door
slam and then the wheels spinning in the dirt. Sixty seconds later, Donald Lucero drove up.

Will walked outside and watched Lucero climb out of
the squad car. The first thing he asked was what had happened to Will's mouth. Will told him that he'd had an
argument with his girlfriend and she'd hit him with an
ashtray. When Will spoke, he could feel his lower lip
stretch tight as if it were too big for his mouth. It was
throbbing some, but there wasn't any pain.

"That's Ray Pacheco's truck," Donald said without
looking at it. He was standing by his car. Will thought
that both the squad car and Donald Lucero in his neat
blue uniform looked weirdly out of place in front of his
house.

"I know that's Ray's truck," he said.

"Where's Ray?" Lucero asked. When he spoke, his
mouth moved but the rest of his face stayed still and
heavy, as if it had been cast that way. Lucero walked over
to Ray's truck, opened the door, and looked inside the
cab. He shut it back up, stared at Will, and asked again,
"Where's Ray?"

"He's at the gorge," Will said. "It happened out
there. I left him and drove back here in his truck."

"What happened out there?"

"He shot himself."

Lucero didn't say anything for a few seconds, and then he asked, "He shot himself how?"

"With a gun. A revolver. Under his chin."

"Who else was with you?"

"Just the two of us."

"Who was the woman who called the dispatcher?"

"A friend. Lisa Segura."

Lucero looked at him for a while longer and then walked over to the squad car. He took some keys out of his pocket and unlocked the back door. He held it open. "Get in," he said.

They drove to the dirt road that led off the highway to the gorge, and Lucero pulled the car onto the shoulder. They sat there without talking, the car engine idling softly. Will wondered what they were waiting for, and he thought that it was good he'd checked Ray for a pulse. If there had been any life left in him, it would have been long gone by now. Will rested his head back against the seat and closed his eyes. The windows were closed, and the air in the car was heavy and hot. Will wondered how his life had come apart so completely in just a few days.

Twenty minutes later, a state trooper showed up along with an ambulance. Lucero must have seen them coming. He sat up straighter in the front seat and pushed the transmission into drive. The car jerked forward and Lucero ended up taking the turn a little too fast, the car scraping dirt, bottoming out hard. Will told him the ruts were bad, and he grunted. He glanced at Will in the mirror and then moved his eyes away. Out the rear window, Will watched the state cop and the ambulance take the turn slowly, the ambulance lurching slightly on the slope down from the highway. Both vehicles had the decency to have their sirens off, but their lights were on and swirling, flashing blue and red in the dust that Lucero's vehicle had kicked up.

Ray was where Will had left him, but he wasn't alone, and Will thought that he'd been stupid not to have covered the body with something. A dozen or so large black ravens stood around Ray. They flew off squawking when Lucero approached and then lit down in the sage fifty yards away. Lucero jumped out of the car quickly and yelled, waving his arms. He picked up a rock and threw it. The birds flew up in the air a few feet, there was the heavy sound of their wings beating air, and then they settled back down where they had been. Lucero picked up another rock and threw it, but this time they ignored him altogether. He came back to the car, unlocked the door, and motioned Will out.

"You shouldn't have left him here like that," he said and walked away.

Will stayed by the car and watched the four of them, Lucero, the state trooper, and the two guys from the ambulance, a couple of tall, rangy Anglos in blue jeans and white shirts, walk up to Ray. Lucero said, "Jodido birds," and the state cop said something that made the two EMTs laugh. Lucero shook his head and didn't say anything else.

The wind was still blowing, but it wasn't gusting as it had been earlier. The sun, as hot as ever, was perched just above the horizon. Will could taste the bitter residue of whiskey in the back of his mouth. When he swallowed, the saliva went down his throat like mud. His lip hurt only when he moved it, but then it felt as though it were going to split open. He rubbed his chin and his hand came away with some dry flakes of blood.

One of the EMTs knelt down next to Ray and did what Will had done earlier, put his fingers against Ray's neck and kept them there, checking for a pulse. After a moment, he stood up and looked back down at Ray with the other three. "Surprise, surprise," he said. "Do you want us to take him now?"

The state cop nodded slowly, his jaw moving as if there were something in his mouth. "Sure," he said. "Go ahead."

The EMTs walked back to the ambulance. Lucero and the state trooper stared at Ray for a while longer, and then Lucero branched away slowly, his head bent, his eyes scanning the ground as though looking for clues. Will took out a cigarette, lit it, and stuck it in his mouth where it didn't hurt. He watched the state cop come back from his car and put Ray's gun in a clear plastic bag. He sealed the bag, took it to his squad car, and tossed it on the front seat.

The EMTs dragged a stretcher from the back of the ambulance and carried it over. They laid it on the ground next to the body, and, with one guy taking Ray's feet and the other his arms, they loaded the body onto the stretcher. When they lifted him, Ray's body sagged in the middle, his butt scraping the ground, and Will could hear the guy who had Ray's arms grunt trying to lift him higher. Ray's head tilted forward and two red lines of fresh blood ran from his hairline down each side of his nose and dripped in a steady stream off his chin onto his shirt. His eyes were open and he looked dazed, as though he weren't exactly sure what had happened. His face was pale and drawn, the flesh sagging, and he looked older and used up, which, Will thought, he was. When they dropped Ray heavily onto the stretcher, his head fell back so that Will couldn't see his face. They carried the stretcher over to the ambulance, slid it into the back, and then climbed in the front seat.

The state trooper waved his hand absently, and the ambulance drove off. Will could picture Ray tossing around in back when the vehicle hit the ruts, his head moving from side to side, his eyes open and confused. There was a dark wet spot on the ground where he had lain, probably soaked through enough to be mud. Beyond that, in the sage, Ray's hat moved gently in the breeze.

Lucero and the trooper walked over to Will, Lucero trailing behind a little. The trooper walked with a bit of a swagger, his arms away from his body. The name plate on his chest read "L. Quintana." He stopped in front of Will and took a few seconds to look at him.

"Your lip could use a stitch," he said. "Did Mr. Pacheco do that to you?"

"No," Will said. "It happened later. It didn't have anything to do with this."

"You tripped and fell?"

"I told Donald already. I had a fight with my girl-friend."

"Over what?" he asked, and suddenly Will could see the conversation going in a direction that made him feel uneasy.

Will shrugged. "Over nothing," he said. "I don't know. We fight."

L. Quintana looked over at Lucero. "His mouth was bleeding when I picked him up," Lucero said. "It looked like it had just happened."

"Do you know this girl?" Quintana asked him. Lucero nodded and said that he knew the family. Quintana brushed at something on the side of his face. "Well, Bill," he said, and Will didn't bother to correct him, "Why don't you tell us what happened out here?"

Will took a deep breath and let it out slowly. Then he began. Lucero never said a word. Quintana interrupted every once in a while with a question. He asked Will what time it was when he and Ray left his house. How long they'd driven around town. Where they stopped. What time it was when Will returned to Guadalupe alone. Had he touched Ray's revolver, and had either one of them been drinking?

When Will had finished, Quintana waited as if there were more to say. He took off his hat and brushed at his hair with his fingers. He put his hat back on, puffed out his cheeks, and blew out some air. "Are you related to Mr. Pacheco?" he asked.

"No," Will said. "We're not related."

The sun dipped below the horizon and all of a sudden the air stilled, not a breath of breeze, as though the sun had taken the wind with it when it set. A fly buzzed Quintana's face and he waved at it.

"Were you friends?" he asked.

Will, and probably even Donald Lucero, who stood mute a few yards away, knew what Quintana was asking. And for a moment Will almost spilled it out, almost told L. Quintana that the reason Ray picked him up wasn't due to friendship but because Ray couldn't stand the sight of him, that if there were an afterlife, Ray would be pleased to see Will standing here in the sagebrush with a couple of cops, faced with the dismal prospect of returning to Guadalupe. Will didn't know what stopped him. He didn't know why it seemed smarter not to get involved in explaining the mess everything had become since Felipe told him about the girl on the bridge. But he didn't take the time to think about it. He shied away as if he were leaning back from a railing at a great height. He wasn't sure why he pulled away. He just did.

He looked at Quintana. The fly came back, if it was the same one, and buzzed the air between them. Will swatted it aside, in Lucero's direction.

"I talked to Ray a couple of days ago," Will said. "About an old truck he had junked. When he came over this afternoon and asked me to take a drive, I thought that was what it was about. We started driving around, talking, drinking some, and somehow we ended up out here. Ray was pretty drunk. He told me he had cancer and that he didn't want to live that way. We got out and walked over to where you could see the river. The next thing I know, Ray has a gun in his hand, and then it's under his chin. I didn't even have time to move. He pulled the trigger and fell." Will moved his eyes away from Quintana. The spot where Ray had fallen was drying up, and beyond that he could see the flock of ravens still standing around, waiting for them to leave. Ray's hat had fallen from the sage and was lying in the dirt.

When Will brought his eyes back, Quintana was looking at Lucero. "Damn," he said, "it's dry out here."

"Always," Lucero said.

Quintana flipped over his wrist and looked at his watch. He looked back at Lucero. "I don't see any reason to take Bill in, do you?"

Lucero stared at Will for a moment. Finally, he shrugged. "I don't have any say out of the village limits."

Quintana grunted and turned back to Will. "How long have you lived here?" he asked.

"Eighteen, nineteen years."

"Do you own property?"

"Yes. A house and some land in Guadalupe."

Quintana looked at Lucero and raised his eyebrows. "Is this true?" he asked.

"As far as I know," Donald said, "what he says is true."

Quintana made a ticking sound with his tongue. After a few seconds, he said, "Okay, Bill, Officer Lucero can give you a ride back home. Thanks for your help. I'll tell the medical examiner you're available at the number you gave me. Is there any problem with that?"

"No," Will told him.

"Do you have transportation to get to his office if he needs to see you?"

"Yes."

Quintana nodded slowly and then gave a slight shrug. "That's it, fellas. You guys can head out."

They drove off, leaving Quintana sitting alone in his squad car, his hat off, one hand moving idly through his hair, the other filling out forms.

Lucero didn't say a word on the ride back. Will sat in the back seat watching the mountains fill up the front windshield, growing larger as they drove east. There wasn't much daylight left when they came to the highway, and Donald switched on the headlights. They drove south into town. Felix's was closed down for the night, hardly any traffic at all on the road. Sunday night. Everyone smart was home resting up for Monday morning.

Ray's truck was gone from Will's house. Lucero told him that a wrecker had come and towed it off. He climbed out of the car and let Will out of the back seat. Lucero looked as though he wanted to say something, but whatever it was, he kept it to himself. He got back in the squad car and drove off slowly, the sound of stones beneath his tires. Will watched the taillights swing down the road and behind the trees and disappear altogether. Then he turned and looked at his house. He thought that it seemed larger to him in the dark, unfamiliar, as though something had changed while he was gone.

Eleven

L ATE ONE AUTUMN,
Telesfor Ruiz had told Will the story of his father's death.
The leaves had turned but had not yet fallen, and the
scrub oak on the foothills was burnt red. The aspens
higher up were the color of gold. It was a still, warm day,
but beneath it was the feel of another season. Will had listened as Telesfor spoke of his father and the tree that had
killed him, but in his mind, along with Telesfor's story, he
heard his own.

Will had been raised in a place where the country was
flat and never changing and where the sky always seemed
to be a different shade of gray. His father, who was quiet
and good natured and who mistakenly thought that he
would get somewhere in his life if he just placed one foot
in front of the other, day after day, had died not long before Will came to Guadalupe.

He died when the tractor he was riding reared up like
an animal one spring morning, throwing him to the
ground and snapping the small bones in his neck. Will's
father had lain there alone for hours without the ability to

move, and all he could see with one open eye was the ground he had just plowed.

Late in the day, Will found his father lying in the fields. His father's eyes had remained open in death, and his face was pressed into the earth. Will knelt down and lifted his father's head and brushed the dirt from his face. He said his father's name aloud and then in a whisper. And in that moment, he felt far older than the man he was holding.

Will said none of these things to Telesfor. He only listened as Telesfor's story and his own wove through his mind. When the old man finished speaking, he pushed himself up from the table and walked stiffly to the window and stood there gazing out at the foothills. In the silence between them, Will asked what Telesfor thought his mother knew about her husband's death that no one else did.

Without turning, Telesfor said that his mother had always been a religious woman. He had heard stories from his grandmother that even as a child his mother had dressed her dolls as if they were saints. She would take them to mass on Sunday and sit them in a row beside her, a thing, his grandmother had said, that always confused the priest. When she was grown and married, his mother no longer kept dolls but santos of Our Lady of Guadalupe, and although these things held little interest for her husband, she believed their presence kept her family from harm.

One winter, at the urging of the priest, who thought that God should remain in the church, not in his parishioners' kitchens, Telesfor's father removed all of the Ladies and placed them in a shed, where they stood by themselves looking out over fields of snow. Soon after, Telesfor's grandmother fell ill and did not recover, and the summer that followed brought with it his father's death. Telesfor's mother knew in her heart that when she allowed her husband to remove the Ladies, she had lost her family.

Will woke feeling as though he hadn't slept but had spent the night in a coma. It was seven A.M. and the sun was shining in the window. He rolled over onto his side, his lip throbbed softly against the pillow, and he could feel a pulsing behind his eyes that he knew would turn into a headache. Shadows of dreams stirred in his head. There was nothing vivid enough for him to draw on, but there was enough to bring back the sight of large black birds flapping their wings and Ray lying in the dirt in the midst of them.

"You shouldn't have left him here like that," Donald Lucero had said. Will shut his eyes and groaned.

If the phone hadn't rung in the kitchen, Will might have tried to block out the entire day and stayed in bed. He managed to get to the phone by the third ring. When he picked up the receiver, whoever was on the other end of the line said, "You're a dead man, jodido," and then there was just the soft click as he hung up. Will put the phone down, walked over to the door, and looked out at nothing. He realized that he had absolutely no idea what to do about anything.

Lloyd Romero was skulking around outside the lumber-yard when Will pulled in. Even before Will shut off the engine, he could see Lloyd moving toward him. He knew how much it took to get Lloyd out of the café before eight A.M. Here we go, he thought. The front door to the store was propped open, and Will could see Joe and Lawrence inside, talking at the front counter. Lloyd cut the distance quickly, angling to head Will off at the door as though if he didn't make it, he might tackle Will from behind. Will slowed down to let him catch up.

"What's this I hear?" Lloyd said, puffing a little bit from his sprint. He was standing on the cement walk, which made him and Will nearly the same height.

Will took a deep breath and widened his eyes, stretch-ing the skin on his face. "I'm running late, Lloyd," he said and took the step up. Lloyd grabbed his arm just above the elbow.

"What the hell you shoot Ray Pacheco for?"

Will stopped walking. "What are you talking about?" he said. "I didn't shoot Ray. He shot himself."

Lloyd's fingers clenched a little tighter, and he pulled Will's arm to his chest. "I've known that asshole my whole life. He was too mean to shoot himself. What hap-pened out there?" Will noticed that Lloyd couldn't keep his eyes off his bruised lip.

"I was just along for the ride, Lloyd," he said. "The man was sick with cancer and depressed as hell about it." He pulled his arm away, and Lloyd's arm came along with it. "Lloyd," Will said, "I got to go."

"So what's all this about Ray raping some hippie girl from Canto Rodado?"

Will felt as though he'd been hit in the stomach. "What?" he said.

Lloyd let go of his arm, reached in his pocket, and took out a cigarette. He stuck it between his teeth and wobbled it up and down, grinning. "I hear," he said, "that you got pictures of Ray putting it to some white girl."

"That isn't right, Lloyd. I don't know who you've been talking to, but Ray was sick. Real sick. And I don't know anything about any pictures."

Joe walked out of the lumberyard. He stood in the sun, squinting, his hands in his pockets.

Lloyd lit up his cigarette. "That's not what I hear," he said.

Will looked over at Joe. "Joe," he said. "Has Felipe been here?"

"He came in early, Will. He was here when I opened up. Got a load and took off."

"What's Felipe got to do with this?" Lloyd said.

"Nothing, Lloyd," Will said. He thought that if he had a stick in his hands he could pound Lloyd over the head with it. He looked back at Joe. "You got any coffee inside?"

A pickup pulled in and parked in front of the three of

them. The windows were tinted and Will could see only the glare of the sun off the windshield. Joe turned his head toward Will.

"No, Will," he said. "There's no coffee."

"So," Lloyd said loudly, "if nothing happened out there, how come your lip's like that?"

"Never mind my lip," Will said. "I got to go."

"Hey," Lloyd called after him. "Ray was always a sonofabitch. If you were family or one of his friends, you could crap in the road and he'd drive around you. Come over to my place later, Will. We'll talk about this. You need help, you know where I am."

Three miles south of Guadalupe, up on a wooded mesa, Will turned east onto a long, winding private drive. It was narrow and graveled smooth. Tall piñon and scrub oak pushed in on both sides. Will could see fresh tire tracks. By now, Felipe had probably unloaded his truck and was stringing lines for the redwood deck they were to build.

A little way in, Will began to lose his breath. He slowed down and then stopped in the middle of the road. He shut off the engine and rested his forehead on the steering wheel. Outside the cab, there wasn't a sound, only a heavy stillness. Will watched his stomach and chest rise and fall too quickly, as if there weren't enough air for his lungs to swallow. For the first time, he realized that if it hadn't been for him, Ray would still be alive. He thought that when Ray had raised the gun and placed it under his chin, Will's own hand had rested like a shadow on Ray's, and the two of them together had pulled the trigger.

Felipe had just finished shoveling the load of sand and gravel out of the back of his truck and was drinking a cup of coffee when he heard the sound of a vehicle. Will's pickup swung slowly around the last curve before the house and came to a stop a few yards away from him.

Out the open window of the truck, Will said, "I thought you'd be done by now."

There was an ashen color to Will's face, and Felipe thought the words that came out of Will's mouth trembled slightly. He grunted. "I didn't expect to see you today," he said.

Will shook his head. "Next time I ask you to tell me any more stories, tell me to shut up."

Felipe drank some of his coffee. "I had a nice weekend," he said. "I went fishing with the boys, and it didn't matter that we caught nothing. Last night I fell asleep watching TV." Will could see that Felipe's eyes were clear, his face smooth and unlined. He looked as though he'd slept like a baby. "I hear," Felipe went on, "you went fishing out at the river with Ray. You catch your lip on a hook?"

"What did you hear?" Will asked.

Felipe had heard the story the night before when Lisa had called Elena. He had been sitting quietly in the open doorway of his house, drinking a beer and looking at the shadows of his garden, when the phone rang. He had sat there listening to Elena's voice grow more and more animated, thinking that he didn't even want to know what she was hearing. When she hung up the phone, she walked through the house and stood behind him. She cleared her throat, and Felipe knew her hands were on her hips and she was not smiling. "I just heard," she said, "that your stupid friend got Ray Pacheco shot, and now the whole village wants to kill him." Felipe didn't say anything. He moved his eyes away from his garden and stared straight ahead at nothing. "I just want to know," Elena went on, "what kind of things you've been telling him for this to happen."

"I heard enough," Felipe said now. He thought that Will looked as though he hadn't slept in days and that his lip was too big for his mouth. He tossed the rest of his coffee on the ground. "It's been nice working with you," he said and walked to the back of the truck and began dragging out the bags of cement.

Will got out of the truck and walked over to Felipe. He leaned against the side of the pickup. "This will blow over," he said.

Felipe tossed the last bag on the ground. "Sure it will," he said.

"I'm not going anywhere," Will said.

"Good." He bounced a wheelbarrow out of the bed.

"Maybe you can change your name," he said. "Grow a beard."

"This isn't my fault," Will said, although there was little of him that believed it.

Felipe moved toward Will. "Out of the way," he said. He took out a couple of shovels and a pick and put them in the wheelbarrow.

"You think it's that bad?" Will asked.

Felipe ran his hand across his forehead and then through his hair. "You think it can get any worse, jodido? In a long weekend, you have made the whole town mad and somehow managed to get Ray killed. Who cares whose fault it is? You stuck a stick in a hole, and now you're surprised you got bit. Do I think it's that bad?" He blew out a mouthful of air. "If it was me, I'd be home packing."

"Lloyd said if I needed help to go get him."

Felipe snorted. "Lloyd," he said. "Lloyd likes you on Monday, forgets your name on Tuesday. If there's a fight Lloyd's right there yelling, but you watch, he never gets hit. What happened to your mouth, anyway?"

"Lisa hit me with an ashtray."

"See. Even your girlfriend's after you."

"This is what happened," Will said.

Felipe held up his hand. "No," he said. "Don't tell me. Lisa called and talked to Elena last night. So I heard some. I don't want to talk about this now."

Will and Felipe had gotten the job through Joe at the lumberyard. He'd told them the owner thought his two-story house looked like a tall cardboard box, which it did, and wanted a deck built on the east side to soften the lines. It was the kind of job both of them liked. At the base of the foothills and for a homeowner who lived somewhere else most of the year and wouldn't be around watching or talking or anything.

Will picked up a shovel, hoping work might chase everything away. It would feel good not to talk and to have the sweat run down his spine and fly from his face when he shook his head. The ground was rocky, and it was all right wrestling stones and dirt out of the holes with the point of the shovel. But after a while, the sun began to burn through his shirt, and the silence in which they were working didn't feel easy. Will's pulse started up again behind his eyelids, and whenever his shovel struck rock, the impact shot up his arms to the base of his skull. By the time they broke for lunch, a quarter of the holes were dug and it seemed to Will as though they'd been working forever.

"I thought he was going to shoot me," Will said, sitting down under a piñon, not far from Felipe. His words sounded empty to him now, like a dream that wasn't even his. He said it again, not just to repeat it but to try to bring it back.

"I thought he was going to shoot me. We got to the river, and I swear all I wanted to do was drink some beers and make hamburgers with Lisa. I knew it was a bad idea to get in his truck, but I climbed in anyway. By the time we got to the river, Ray had finished off the pint. He starts talking about how sick he is and how he and his father spent summers out there grazing sheep. Then, all of a sudden, he's got this gun in his hand. One minute we're looking at the river and the next there's this gun pointed at my face."

"Did your life flash in front of your eyes?" Felipe asked.

Will looked at him for a few seconds. "No, my life didn't flash before my eyes." He wondered how, in the middle of what he was saying, Felipe could ask such a dumb question.

"Ray said, 'Vaya con Dios,'" Will went on, "and then he brought the gun up under his chin and pulled the trigger. There wasn't anything I could do, it happened so fast. He flew backwards and landed flat on his back." Will stopped talking and looked down at the half-eaten peanut-butter-and-jelly sandwich Felipe had given him. He picked it up and took a bite. It tasted as dry as dust, but he swallowed it down. "I never covered him up when I left," he said. "When we got back, the birds were on him."

Felipe was scooping beans and chile out of a bowl with a tortilla. He looked at Will, his jaws chewing. "That probably bothers you the most, doesn't it? When Ray's around, you can't stand him. When he's dead and doesn't care about nothing, you worry about birds." He scooped some more chile out of the bowl and stuck it in his mouth. "If I was Ray," he said, "it's you I would have shot."

"Half the village saw us driving around," Will said. "There's no way he could have shot me and got away with it."

"Who said he wanted to get away with it?" Felipe remembered a day long ago when Melvin Cortéz, a man who was born in a foul mood and who became even worse when he drank, which was always, shot and killed his neighbor. Melvin never told anyone why he did this, saying only that it was nobody's business but his own. As Melvin's second cousin was married to the sister of the judge in Las Sombras, and as the dead man had no family and was new in Guadalupe, this was a trial that never came to be. Felipe thought that it was just Will's good luck that Ray was as sick as he was.

"I think," Will said, "that Ray just wanted to make sure everyone knew I was the reason he shot himself." Will ate some more of his sandwich and washed it down with cold coffee. He was beginning to feel better, but he didn't know whether that was because of the food or sitting out of the sun or just being able to talk about all this instead of having it caged in his head. "Don't Catholics go to hell if they kill themselves?" he asked.

"If Ray had cancer like you say," Felipe said, "he was half dead already. That doesn't make it so bad. It might be harder to explain murder to God. Actually, Ray was pretty smart. He didn't have to stick around and get sick, and he left it so his family will take care of you."

"You think so?"

Felipe took in a deep breath and then belched. "He never had any kids," Felipe said, "but he's got a lot of relatives. Jimmy was mad at you for just talking to Ray. I don't think he's going to be too happy about this. Look, say you've lived your whole life in some little town and some stranger shows up and shoots your father or messes with your sister. You think you'd just forget about it? Hell, Will, you'd go get drunk with your buddies and then cut the guy's balls off. That's what would happen." Felipe shoved the remainder of the tortilla in his mouth and looked past Will. "That house is ugly," he said. "I think all a deck will do is make it look like a cardboard box with a lip."

Will stared at him for a few seconds. "You've got chile all over your face," he said. A yellow jacket buzzed his head. He swatted at it with his hand and it flew off into the woods, droning like a small plane. "I hate those bees. They don't make honey. They don't pollinate anything. They're like flies, but they bite."

"Flies bite," Felipe said.

"Maybe you they bite."

"In the fall they bite. When it starts to get cold. They get mean and want to take it out on something."

"What, you think flies get grouchy? They get chilly, so it's time to chew on something?"

"You ever see flies on a dog's ear? One day they're

just sitting there and the next the ear's all bloody. What do you call that?"

"All right. All right, flies bite. But they're still not as bad as yellow jackets. I don't believe we're talking about this."

Felipe took an orange out of his lunchbox. He peeled it carefully and tossed half to Will. There were dark smudges on it from his fingers. Will stuck a section in his mouth. "So," he said, "what do you think I should do?"

"You ask me this now? Why didn't you ask a few days ago when you thought it was such a good idea to go visit Ray?" Felipe spit out an orange seed. "Maybe you should leave for a little while." Like twenty years, Felipe thought, though he didn't say it.

"Leave? Where am I going to go?"

Felipe shrugged. "Then stay and see what happens. Someone's going to mess with you, though. Don't think it won't happen. Tonight, tomorrow, sometime."

Will ate the rest of the orange and slumped down lower against the tree. He took out a cigarette and lit it. "The funny thing," he said, "is I got to like Ray since he's been dead." Between the branches of the tree, Will could see two hawks gliding high up.

"You got to like the girl, too," Felipe said, "and she's been dead for twenty-five years. Maybe you just like dead people, Will."

By late afternoon, when they had finished digging, Will could feel a nagging ache in the small of his back and blisters beneath the calluses on his palms. It seemed hotter than ever. The sun was still high, and although Will had thought his arms were as dark as they could get, he could feel a burn under his skin.

They tossed the shovels into Felipe's truck and went over to the shady side of the house. Will turned on the spigot and let the water run through the hose until it cooled. There was a faint taste of plastic to it, but he drank until he could feel the water sloshing around in his stomach. Felipe took the hose and ran water over the back of his neck and then let the nozzle rest on the inside of each wrist. "It cools the blood this way," he had once told Will, "so your heart doesn't go into shock." When he finished, Will took the hose back and washed off his arms and drank a little more.

"You drink too much, you'll get sick."

"You think I'm one of your kids, don't you?" Will threw the end of the hose onto some sad-looking sod and let the water run. "We could stay late," he said. "Get a little more done."

"I can't stay late," Felipe said, wiping water and some of the day's dirt from his face with his shirt. "There's a rosary for Ray tonight. At seven. Elena warned me to be home on time."

Will didn't say anything for a moment. He looked at Felipe until Felipe moved his eyes away. A rosary for Ray, Will thought. "You're going?" he asked.

"I've known Ray all my life, Will. His wife is first cousins with Elena's mother. Yes, I'm going. Maybe instead of hiding in your house, you should come along."

Will pictured himself kneeling in church while the priest led the rosary. After that, he would stand in line with everyone while they circled the aisles and gave their condolences to the family. He saw himself patting Jimmy on the shoulder. Will took in a deep breath and let it out slowly. "I don't think that's a good idea," he said. "I should probably go see Lisa, anyway."

"She'll be at the church."

"Lisa?"

Felipe shrugged. "Maybe not," he said. "She and Lalo were classmates, though. This could be a big rosary. Ray knew a lot of people. And even if they didn't like him, they'll still come to say good-bye and give their best to his wife. If you come, maybe no one will even notice you."

"I'm not sure I believe that."

"You can sit with us, jodido. Elena won't let anyone hurt you. You can wait outside when everyone goes up to the family. Maybe if you don't make this into a big deal, no one else will either."

"You think so?"

Felipe went over to the spigot and shut it off. The sod still looked brown and dried out. "No," he said. "You'd stick out like a sore thumb," which was exactly how Will felt, but it didn't make him feel any better to hear it said out loud.

Twelve

WILL'S HOUSE WAS STILL standing when he got home. No one had come over while he was at work with a can of gasoline and a match. He switched off the engine and smoked a cigarette. The sun was falling gently in the west; the rosary for Ray would be beginning soon. It would be hot and crowded in the church with the heavy scent of sweat and perfume. Ray would be laid out in a casket before the altar, dressed in a suit, his face powdered and rouged but still ashen and dead. Kneeling somewhere in the aisles would be Lisa and Felipe. Will flicked his cigarette away and heard the phone begin to ring inside the house. He swung the truck door open and jumped out. He picked up the receiver just in time to hear someone say staccato, "You're dead, jodido. You're dead. You're dead. You're dead." Will hung up. He thought not everyone was heading for church.

He got two more of the same calls in the next thirty minutes. One of them was a kid, his voice still high and smooth. He got excited and began babbling when Will answered. Will let him go on for a few seconds and then cut in, saying he knew who this was and was going to tell his father. That shut the kid up for a moment, and when he said, "You don't know," Will broke the connection. Instead of hanging up, he left the receiver off the hook.

Will took the Lady from the wall along with the two photographs and sat down at the table. He stretched out his legs and leaned back in the chair. Through the open door, he could see the cottonwoods along the creek and the junipers that grew in the shadows of the larger trees. The santo's eyes were open and turned toward him. He could see wood beneath the flaked paint on her gown. Her hands, which were clasped at her chest, had small cracks along the line of each finger. Will thought that although this Lady was very old, there was only youth on her mouth and in her eyes.

Out loud, Will said, "I'm not doing so well."

He lowered his eyes to the photograph of a dead girl who had once been a child and who had slept soundlessly at night and been out of breath when she ran. It seemed that this girl had been in his life for a long time, but it had been just days since he had heard of her, and all he knew was that her life had ended. And that would be all he would ever know. "There's no place for us to go with this," he said. "It has to end here."

He closed his eyes, feeling as though his house was full of women. Although they did not mind his presence, Will knew they would be perfectly happy in only each other's company.

Will dozed until it grew dark. When he finally opened his eyes, he got up from the chair slowly. He went to the phone and dialed Lisa's number. It rang for a long time before Mrs. Segura finally picked it up.

"Could I talk to Lisa?" Will asked.

"She's at the church, don't you know," Mrs. Segura said and hung up. Will knew that the rosary must have ended by now, and he wondered where Lisa had gone. Leaving the phone off the hook again, he put the Lady and the photographs back in the wall and went into his bedroom.

He got the rifle from under the bed and jammed a couple of shells in the magazine. He snapped on the safety and leaned it against the front of the bed, near his pillow. He looked at it leaning there precariously and then laid it down flat on the floor, worried that he might knock it over in his sleep, and then who knew what would happen.

Some part of him heard the vehicle drive up, the soft sound of gravel beneath tires. He heard the door open and then close gently with a click, and he thought it was good that whoever had driven up had the decency to be quiet. He heard footsteps scuffing the ground and then the sharp creak of the kitchen door as it was pushed open. His heart began jumping in his chest. He jerked his head to the side and watched someone walk into the bedroom and then up to the bed. There was the sound of a foot kicking the rifle on the floor and then a grunt that sounded familiar.

"Lisa."

"So now you sleep with guns," she said.

"Turn on the light."

"No," she said, "I'm not staying." She was wearing something white that fell from her shoulders to just below her hips. The only thing Will thought he could see from there down was skin. He couldn't see her features, but from the angle of her head, he knew she was looking down at him. "I dreamed about you," she said.

"In one dream," she went on, "we were by the creek. Not too far from your house. You were smoking a cigarette and giving me a bad time about how even cows were smarter than my brother. Then, like a dream is, I'm far from you, out in the middle of the field, and I see these three men come out of the cottonwoods with knives. Big knives. One of them stabs you hard, here," Lisa poked Will's stomach, "while the other two stand in front trying to hide from me what they are doing to you. The one who stabs you stays bent over you for a long time, and when he gets up, I know in my heart you are dead. That's when I wake up and go to the phone and try to call you, and all I get is a busy signal over and over again. So I go back to bed, and I have a worse dream."

She didn't say anything for a moment. She put her hands on the edge of the bed and brought her face down closer to Will.

"In this dream," she said, "you are in a strange room fucking a gringa. The two of you are having a lot of fun together, and when I walk into this room, you don't even have the good manners to stop." Lisa put her hand on Will's face and moved her fingers around as if she were reading braille. She found his lower lip and pinched it with two fingers, right where she'd bashed him with the ashtray. Then she pulled up slowly until Will's head came off the pillow.

"If you ever do that again," she said; then she gave his lip a last squeeze and let it go. They were silent in the dark. "Don't you forget," she said finally. Then she bent over him so he could feel her hair on his face and kissed the corner of his mouth. "There," she said. "And maybe you should brush your teeth at night, también," and she whirled and walked away.

Will walked around the outside of his house in a still, pale dawn that held enough heat to warn him the day was going to be hot. He moved slowly, sipping coffee and looking at the place as though he'd never seen it before. He saw how the plaster that he'd sworn to redo for the past five years was now so cracked that when he pushed on it with the flat of his hand he could feel it give. Wasp nests, paper and mud, coated the eaves thickly, as if someone had messed up the surface of the wood with a trowel. Birds had worked themselves into the area where wall met roof, and as Will walked by one squeezed itself out and swooped by him, arching high and back over the roof. The whole place was sagging, as though it had given up a long time ago and decided that it would, inch by inch, slide back into the earth.

He went around to the north side of the house to the pile of debris he'd collected over the past eighteen years. Warped lumber, old crates of spikes that had split open, the nails corroded with rust. Ax heads, broken shovels, old handsaws, gallons of linseed oil, busted cinder blocks, a burnt-out tractor engine he'd traded for, although, for the life of him, he couldn't recall why. Box springs, an old oak bureau that the weather had twisted and crippled, bald tires with the wire treads poking through. Cedar posts, coils of barbed wire, a refrigerator that had burned out and only kept things warm. It was an impressive pile, and Will thought that none of it was worth a damn.

He walked back to the front of the house and out into the field. From there, if he blinked his eyes over and over, the house didn't look so bad. But when he stopped blinking, it changed into something as sad and neglected as an old dog kept chained up for too long. He drank the rest of his coffee.

Mañana, he thought. Mañana.

As Will was about to leave the house, the phone rang. Someone named Andrew Martínez was calling from the medical examiner's office in Las Sombras. He apologized for disturbing Will so early but said that he had tried to reach him a number of times the day before with no luck. He was calling to say that the matter of Ray Pacheco's death appeared to be straightforward and that Will would not need to come in and sign a deposition.

Will asked if he was aware of Ray's medical status, and Martínez told him yes, he had received a copy of Ray's medical records from the VA hospital. "These are sad things," Martínez went on. "Especially for the family. I know that what you went through could not have been easy, but maybe it'll be a comfort for Ray's relatives knowing someone was with him when he died."

Thirteen

FELIPE DROVE UP TO the job site at just past six o'clock in the morning. He was two hours earlier than usual, and he knew that Will more than likely wasn't even out of bed yet. He sat in his pickup with the window open, the sun still not above the mountains. He looked at the house and thought that at least there was no homeowner around to pester him, which was about the only good thing he could think of in his life right now. He climbed slowly out of his truck. He was tired, and the muscles in his back were sore from digging the day before. He walked over to the wheelbarrow and looked at it. Felipe was thirty-seven years old. If he felt this bad now, he wondered how he would feel in twenty years.

"I'll be dead," he said out loud, which made him feel a little better. "Somebody else can mix cement and spend their stupid life worrying." As he pushed the wheelbarrow, he kept talking to himself, but he was no longer listening.

The rosary had been a disaster for Felipe. The church had been crowded with people and the air inside, even with the doors left open, was hot and smelled of perfume and sweat and manure from Manuel Gallegos's corral, which was not far away. To Felipe, who sat in the middle of all this, the air was like something that had to be chewed and then swallowed. Halfway through the service, Philistina Hernández, who had been kneeling quietly beside Felipe and who was a large woman and no longer young, rested her hand on his shoulder and whispered, "Hijo, tell Ray to stop singing and waving his hands like that." Felipe saw that her face was like chalk and her eyelids were fluttering. Then she fell heavily against him in a faint. Trying not to fall in turn, Felipe found himself wrestling awkwardly with this woman as if she had attacked him.

Felipe and three other men carried Philistina from the church. Philistina's daughter, Andelma, walked alongside them holding onto the hem of her mother's dress so that it would not rise above her knees, a thing, Andelma knew, that would concern her mother the most when she woke. They laid Philistina in the grass beneath the juniper tree just outside the church doors. As Felipe stood there with the others, looking down at Philistina and breathing air that did not taste like mud, Philistina opened her eyes briefly and moved her lips as if to speak. Andelma stroked her mother's forehead, and Felipe, suddenly afraid of what words might come out of the old woman's mouth, turned and hurried back inside. When he knelt once again beside Elena, she gave him a look that said, "This, too, was your fault."

After Father Roberto, a young priest new to

Guadalupe, finished leading the rosary, Felipe rose and, along with everyone else, waited in line to give his condolences to the family of Ray Pacheco. As he shuffled along behind Elena, he glanced at the open coffin that sat before the altar. Ray's eyes were closed and his face looked as if it had been made out of clay. Felipe thought that not long ago, Ray had been eating chile and tortillas and drinking beer and irrigating his alfalfa with a shovel. It also occurred to him that there was little of Ray left now and that what was left did not look like someone who would be waving his arms and singing. Felipe wondered what had gone through Philistina Hernández's mind just before she fainted. Will would enjoy this story, he thought, and then he chased the idea away. If he was smart, he would never tell Will anything else, ever again.

Bella, Ray's wife, did not look at Felipe when he took her hand and bent low and told her how sorry he was and that if there was anything he could do. She nodded her head and said nothing. Beside her sat her nephew Jimmy, whom Felipe had known all his life. When he took Felipe's hand, he grabbed it tightly and pulled it to his chest, saying only, "When we get him, jodido, you better not be anywhere around."

Felipe and Elena drove home together in silence. As soon as Felipe walked into his house, he went straight to bed. He lay there, staring at nothing and hearing the voices of his children in the next room. He wondered how his life, which he had always thought of as simple and containing only small problems such as tomato plants that did not grow and three children who seemed to enjoy hitting each other continually with sticks, had suddenly become so confusing and humorless. He thought that all this could be blamed on Will, but he knew he had played a part, and for the life of him, he couldn't figure out what it was. It was as if he had kicked a rock down a slope and then watched open mouthed as it flattened chickens and flew through windows and bounced off the head of Ray Pacheco.

Felipe finally fell asleep long after Elena had come to bed. And then, as if things could only become worse, he dreamed. He didn't dream one dream, but hundreds of dreams, and when he woke before dawn, he felt as though he had spent the night running from one thing to another. He lay still in bed and listened to the soft sounds his wife made in her sleep. Outside the open window, he could hear the chirping of a single bird that was probably eating something in his garden. Felipe closed his eyes tight and thought this might be a good day to have nothing to do with.

When Will left the house, he thought he was going to work, but just a little way down the highway, he made a quick right and took the road that led to Lisa's house. He thought he had time for a cup of coffee with her and could still beat Felipe to the job site.

Lisa's car was parked in front of her trailer. Will pulled in next to it and got out. A sprinkler set up in the middle of the corn was overshooting the plants. The water was splashing against the side of the trailer, washing off some of the flakes of brown paint. The plants close to where the water was hitting leaned toward the moisture as though they wished they had feet. Mrs. Segura's truck was parked off to the side of her house, and there was no sign of Mundo's vehicle. The place looked quiet, the curtains pulled close together, not a sound from the dog Will knew was chained up behind the house. Maybe Mundo and his mother had gone out for breakfast together or driven to Las Sombras for groceries. But a better bet, Will thought, was that Mundo was still asleep somewhere and Mrs. Segura was staring out at him from behind the curtains and praying to all the saints that her daughter would come to her senses.

Will climbed up the cinder blocks that Lisa had stacked for steps. Before he could knock, the door swung open. Lisa was naked from the waist up. Her jeans were low on her hips. The top button was undone, and a startling patch of white panties showed there. Will didn't know if he should take the last step forward or back down the steps to his truck. He glanced behind him at the empty yard. Lisa hooked her thumbs in both side pockets and pulled her pants down a little lower. She moved her shoulders back and forth, and her breasts swayed gently. She looked at Will and smiled.

"You know, your mother's right over there," he said. "Probably looking out the window right now."

"You don't think my mother's seen me like this?"

"She hasn't seen me see you like this," Will said, looking over his shoulder again. He thought one of the curtains had moved. "Your brother could drive up at any time," he said, turning back.

"So what are you doing out there?"

"I just came by to say good morning."

"So come in and say it."

"I'm on my way to work, Lisa."

"Work? What are you, crazy?"

"You won't pinch my lip or throw anything?"

Lisa shrugged, and Will watched the motion of her breasts. "I don't promise nothing." She grinned and hooked her index finger at him. "Don't be shy," she said.

"I've never seen that one on the end before," Will said. "Is it a new one?" They were lying on top of the white ruffled bedspread that had been a wedding gift to Lisa's great-grandmother. A soft, cool odor of mothballs clung to the fabric as if woven into it. Lisa had found it packed away in a trunk in one of the sheds, buried beneath years of junk. In the trunk, along with the bedspread, were a wedding dress, a water-stained Bible written in French, and a small pair of red shoes that had shrunk in the dryness and were curled up at the toes. Lisa had told Will that if she ever in this lifetime were foolish enough to marry, she would wear that dress, no matter how worn and yellowed it was. She would wear it proudly in her great-abuela's memory. When Will had asked what she would do with the shoes, Lisa said that if they continued to shrink, she would wear one in each ear.

Their legs were sprawled across the bed. Will's head was against the headboard in an angle that strained the muscles in his neck. He could smell, mixed with the odor of mothballs, the scent of sweat and sex and a little bit of Felix's Café. He thought that by now, Felipe must surely be at the job site, shoveling cement and muttering to himself. Lisa rolled off him and propped herself up on her elbows. "Which one is new?" she said.

"The one on the left, on the end. The one that looks like he wants to hide."

"That's not hiding," she said. "That's humility." She let herself fall back down on the bed, twisting some so her head landed on Will's shoulder. "Hiding," she said. "That shows what you know. He was in back. I moved him so he could see things."

The wall opposite the bed was lined with statues of Saint Francis that varied in size. Some were a foot high. Some as tall as four feet. Some of them held bowls for water. Others had their hands cupped before them. A few were carved out of cedar, their features square and garishly painted, others molded gently out of clay or plaster. One was cut out of steel and badly rusted, his flat feet welded onto a steel plate so he wouldn't fall over. There must have been twenty-five of them, crowded around the foot of the bed as though they wanted to climb in. Most of them smiled softly, but a couple of the carved ones had a hint of the conquistador about them. As though, Will thought, they might be more concerned with eating than feeding.

Lisa had gathered these things for years, since child-hood, and when Will first saw them standing at the foot of her bed, what he thought was not that the woman he had just met was slightly unbalanced, though he now thought this was half true, but that in the wall of his house was buried a santo of Our Lady of Guadalupe. He didn't know why he had kept this from Lisa, but he knew that if she found out, of all things that he might do, she would find this the hardest to forgive.

"I don't know how you sleep with all of them in here," Will said.

"They don't make noise."

"They were cheering a little while ago."

"Ha."

Will worked his way a little higher up the headboard. Lisa made a moaning sound, and her head slid down to his stomach. He moved her hair from behind her neck and felt the moisture on her skin. "How was work yester-day?" he asked.

"Eee," she said, "don't even ask." Her mouth was against his skin and her words were muffled. She raised her head a few inches. "A hundred boy scouts came in in two big buses. You know what boy scouts tip? Nothing, that's what. And you would think with the stupid cos-tumes they wear that they would be neat. Pepe cooked a hundred orders of French toast, and for the rest of the day he was in a bad mood." Lisa took some of Will's skin into her mouth and bit down hard enough that he thought she might bite through. "One of those boys was so cute, though. And quiet. Like you would be if you were little again." She lifted her head slightly, taking Will's skin with it, and then let go. She rubbed the teeth marks with her hand and then gave his stomach a slap.

"You should go," she said.

"Go? Go where?"

"To work. Before Felipe comes here looking for you. I can see you later at the baseball game."

"There's a baseball game tonight?" Will said. "You were calling me crazy not so long ago, and now you're throwing me out."

"That was before. You're no good to me now. Maybe if you go shovel some and make me laugh watching you run after a ball, we can eat that hamburger that's rotting in your fridge afterwards and then see what's what." She climbed over him and got off the bed. She stood looking down at him with her hands on her hips.

"I'm going to take a shower," she said. She stayed by the bed for a few more seconds, smiling, and then waved her fingers at him, turned, and walked out of the room.

When Will finally got to the job site, it was nearly eleven and Felipe was mixing cement. His mood had gone from bad to foul. Will stopped the truck alongside him and shut off the ignition. The heat from the engine washed against Felipe's bare arms and over his face.

"It's hot," Will said from inside the cab.

Felipe grunted and kept mixing. "How would you

know?" he said. "You drive around in your truck all morning with the breeze hitting you. And then when we get paid, you still want half the money."

Will could see that the redwood for the deck was stacked neatly against the side of the house. "When did Joe get here with the lumber?" he asked.

"He came so long ago it was like yesterday," Felipe said. He thought that not only was Will three hours late, but when he did show up all he had to say were things that not even a cow would say. A part of him wished that Will had just stayed away and left him alone to enjoy his bad mood by himself.

Will climbed out of the truck. He stood next to the wheelbarrow and watched Felipe push the cement back and forth with his shovel. "You remember that time Octaviano broke his arm and you took three days off? I didn't complain, and that was a plaster job."

"What plaster job?"

"The one for that lady outside Las Sombras. The one who had all those goats."

"Oh, that lady. No wonder you didn't complain. She fed you cookies all day and wore those plastic pants."

"You liked those plastic pants as much as I did."

Felipe grunted. "That was two years ago, jodido. Besides, it wasn't this hot then."

An hour later, Felipe ate his lunch under a piñon tree while Will worked the shovel and wheelbarrow, filling the forms with cement. At one point, Felipe yelled at him, his mouth full of food, "You know, it's strange, but I sit just a few feet away and I feel cool in the shade when I watch you sweating like a horse." Just watching Will work while he sat and rested had made Felipe feel better. "It's like we're in different worlds," he said. He thought that when he was done eating, he would lie back and take a nap.

Will emptied the wheelbarrow and sat down next to Felipe. He wiped the perspiration from his face with the front of his shirt. "It's too hot," he said. "How was the rosary?"

Felipe thought that at Ray's rosary, the corpse had been seen singing and Ray's nephew had said in so many words that Will wouldn't be around much longer. But he only shrugged. "It was like any other rosary," he said and looked away.

Will stretched out on the ground. He could feel pine needles and small stones poking through the shirt into his back. "I thought about that girl last night," he said. "And I realized there was nothing I could do. I guess there was never anything to do. Maybe it would have been nice to know her name. For somebody to know her name."

"Maybe she didn't have a name," Felipe said. He watched an ant climb up one side of his leg. When it got to his thigh, he flicked it away with his finger.

"She was just there," Will said. "And never anywhere else. Her whole life was on the bridge." He didn't say anything for a moment, and then he said, "Did you know that the black man's name was Madewell Brown?"

Will's eyes were closed. Felipe could see a scattering of gray in his hair and wrinkles fanning out from his eyes, from crowding forty and a lifetime of squinting away from the sun. "Qué Madewell Brown?" Felipe said.

"He was here years ago," Will said. "He lived in an old adobe he made his own. And when he left Guadalupe, inside the house were painted thousands of pictures of his children. The whole village went to this house to see these things. Later the place was torn down, and everything Madewell Brown left here disappeared. But he was here once."

Felipe stared down at Will. There was still food in his mouth, but he had stopped chewing. "Where'd you hear this story?" he asked.

"Telesfor Ruiz told me."

For a moment, Felipe had no idea who Telesfor Ruiz was, and then he remembered the way one remembers a shadow. He remembered him only as an old man and nothing else. "How come you never told me this?" he said.

Will opened his eyes and pushed himself up slowly. "What's to tell?" he said. "Telesfor was my neighbor when I first came here. He was dead for years when I met you. I only think of him sometimes." Will got to his feet. "I'll tell you, though, if you ever want to cook a sheep's head, I know how."

They finished pouring the cement around four o'clock. Both of them were beginning to drag with the heat, especially Felipe, who felt like he'd worked a full day before Will had even shown up. The forms were full of cement, an anchor bolt set in each one and the tops troweled smooth. They scattered the leftover sand and gravel in some of the deeper holes in the driveway and then strung out the hose away from the house and washed everything clean. They tossed the tools and the wheelbarrow in the back of Felipe's truck and then stood looking at their work.

Felipe let out a breath of air. "There," he said. "The rotten part's done."

"You think we can get it built tomorrow?"

"If you come on time." Felipe looked at Will. "You coming to the game later?"

"Yeah, I'm going to meet Lisa there. Five-thirty, right?"

"That's right," Felipe said, and suddenly he didn't feel so tired. It would be a good night to hit a stupid baseball and drink a few beers. He smiled and slapped Will on the shoulder. "See you soon, Will," he said.

Fourteen

THE FIELD WAS CROWDED with people and vehicles when Will arrived a little after five. The game hadn't started yet. It seemed to Will that a lot more people were hanging about than usual, as though the whole village had spent the day inside waiting for things to cool off and needed some air now. It didn't feel much cooler, but if you weren't actually out on the field, Will thought, it would be a good evening to sit under the cottonwoods and drink some beer and think about nothing.

He drove his truck past the vehicles lining the outfield, hitting the brakes hard once when a group of small children darted in front of him heading who knew where. A woman sitting in the back of a pickup so the bed faced the field yelled out sharply, "Carlos, you watch out." She turned back to her friends and said, "No," loudly, and then, as if something had hooked her brain, she looked back at where the kids had been and yelled out, "Carlos, I mean it." She smiled at Will and shrugged and turned away.

He swung off the road that would have taken him to his house and drove down the right-field line, the road mazing through cottonwoods. There were cars and trucks parked at angles and shaded by the trees. He pulled to a stop alongside Felipe's truck. Elena was inside the cab with Octaviano and one of Joe Vigil's boys. Will could see the boys from the chin up. Their heads were turned together and both of their mouths were moving. He got out of his pickup and leaned on the hood.

"It's not so bad here in the shade," he said.

Elena was slouched down in the cab. She had one arm dangling out the window, and her head was resting on the edge of the seat. "It doesn't seem cool to me," she said and rolled her head toward the kids. "Because of you two with your stupid talk about your stupid baseball cards."

Octaviano piped out in a high voice, "They're not baseball cards."

Elena raised her voice. "Baseball, football, beach ball, I don't care. Go. Get out. Go find your brothers and give me some peace." She kept her head turned toward them until they finally stopped complaining and climbed out of the truck. "And stay out of the creek," she said. "Or you know what." She looked back at Will. "There, that's a little better. I don't know why boys are so noisy. I'm one of seven girls, and I swear our house was so quiet."

Will smiled and looked past the outfield to where a couple of trucks were creeping in. "There's a lot of people here," he said.

"Boredom," Elena answered. "And too much heat." After a few seconds, she added, "So where's Lisa?"

Will pushed off the hood of his truck. "She should be here soon."

"Are you all right, Will?"

"Yes," he said. "Things got messed up, but everything's all right now."

Elena stared at him quietly, and then she too smiled. "Sure," she said. "I think that if you were in the cab of my truck with my Octaviano and Joe's boy, you'd fit right in. Go play your game so I can watch something."

There was only the semblance of two teams in Guadalupe. One was the loose group of guys Will played with. That included Felipe; Albert and Rudy Durán, who made adobe bricks on their uncle's land; Juanito García, sort of a plumber; and others who did a little bit of everything. The other team was the eight brothers from the lumberyard and their cousins, all of whom seemed to be six feet tall with thick arms and fast hands. There was never much question as to who would win each game, but, as Rudy once said, "We don't play to win, jodido. We play to see if there is a God."

The lumberyard was playing catch on the first-base side, and as Will walked across the infield, Joe caught the ball thrown by his brother Lawrence and raised his glove in a slight wave. Behind home plate and by himself, Lloyd Romero was holding a beer and staring at a small plastic clicker in his hands as if it had just fallen from the sky. As Will walked by, he looked up and said, "You know how this thing works?"

"What is it?"

"It's a thing that tells me the balls and the strikes and the outs. So I don't have to use my fingers."

"You're the umpire?"

"You have a problem with that?"

"No," Will said.

"Good," Lloyd said and looked down at the thing in his hand. "Go tell your team that never wins we're going to start soon."

Will's team was standing around in a loose circle under a cottonwood that spread enough shade to cover all of third base. Their gloves, along with a number of empty beer cans, were thrown off to the side. Rudy, who was Albert's older brother and stood a compact five foot four inches, was in the center of the circle. He was wearing a dust-colored T-shirt that Will thought might have been gray, and there was a bandage on his right arm that ran from his wrist to his elbow.

When Rudy saw Will walking over, he pointed his beer and said, "Fuck no. Put Will on third base. I'm injured. I'll play right field. I'm not playing third base."

"I play right field," Felipe said.

"I don't care where you play," Rudy said. "I'll play out there with you. Will, you play third base."

Will got a beer out of one of the coolers. "Not me," he said and took a long drink. "I barely play this game at all."

"Who cares if you can play this game, jodido? None of us can play this game. All you got to do is stand there."

"What happened to your arm?" Will asked.

Rudy stood with his arm held out from his body. They all looked at it, the bandage stained and dirty, and Will could see that everyone except Rudy was smiling. Rudy shook his head slowly and blew air out of his mouth. "A qué jodido," he said. "A pig is what happened to my arm." He raised his arm up higher. "I almost got it chewed off."

Juanito laughed and then choked on his beer and began coughing. Albert, built like his brother but six inches taller, said, "His pig tried to kill him."

"Qué kill me?" Rudy said and then he looked down at the ground. "My pig tried to eat me."

"They had a pig party Sunday," Felipe said to Will. "But they waited until Sunday morning to kill the pig."

"We were all there," Albert said, looking around. "Well, you weren't there, Will. Neither was Felipe. But the rest of us."

"I came by later," Felipe said. "After the tragedy," and Juanito began laughing again.

Albert smiled at Will. "This was Rudy's pig we were going to butcher, and Rudy didn't want this pig to see him have anything to do with it. So he's out standing by the car, far enough away that he can see what's happening but where the pig won't recognize him. Everyone else is over by the house getting the fire ready. So me and Juanito let this pig out."

"How come you didn't just shoot him in the pen?" Will asked.

Rudy raised his head. "What?" he said. "And let the

other pigs know what's going to happen to them?" He shook his head. "Jodido Will," he said.

Will looked at Albert. "You didn't have a rope around this pig?"

"Hey," Felipe said. "Listen to the story and be quiet."

"Who would think that this pig was like this?" Albert said. "So we open the gate, and we think this pig will wander out like any other pig, and when he does, Juanito will shoot him. But this pig doesn't do that. This pig runs out like he's waited his whole life for this day. He runs right at Rudy, who's out in the driveway all sad because this is his favorite pig. When Rudy sees the pig running straight at him, he screams because he thinks Juanito will miss the pig and shoot him. So Rudy starts running around the side of the car. We think that the pig is going to run for freedom, that Rudy standing there is just an accident. But this pig takes off around the car fast, fast after Rudy. Rudy stops being scared of the gun and starts yelling, 'Shoot him, shoot him, shoot him.'"

Will looked at Juanito. "I was laughing so hard," Juanito said, "that I dropped the gun."

Albert went on, "When Rudy gets to the front of the car, he tries to climb up on the hood, and the pig catches up to him and jumps him from behind and bites his arm."

Will looked at Rudy, who was still looking at the ground, and then back at Albert. He felt a grin grab hold of his face. "You got to be kidding me," he said.

"I fed this fucking pig," Rudy said, "since it was a little pigling."

"That must not be all you did to it," Felipe said.

Lloyd suddenly yelled from home plate that it was getting late and that he had better things to do.

"Esperate, jodido," Rudy yelled at him.

"Just then," Albert said, "my mother and my Tía Rose come out of the house, and they see Rudy screaming and hitting this pig in the head with his hat, and they can see that Rudy's other arm is in the pig's mouth. My mother yells for me to get the ax, and the pig, like he knows Spanish, suddenly lets go of Rudy's arm and starts running. We had to shoot him way out in our neighbor's field and carry him all the way back."

Rudy shook his head. He looked up at Will and held his arm up so Will could see the bandage. "Jodido pig," he said.

Felipe got to play right field alone. Albert put Will in center, and Rudy, even after all his whining, ended up on third. As Will and Felipe were walking out slowly under the sun, Will asked how bad Rudy's arm really was. Felipe laughed and said, "Some punctures. Not real bad. His arm's all blue, though. I think he wears the bandage as a memory to his pig."

Things didn't get better for Rudy. The first batter for the lumberyard hit a screeching line drive down the third-base line that short-hopped Rudy and smacked him square on his bandaged arm. He threw his glove in the air, screamed, and dropped to the ground, squirming in the dirt. When he got back on his feet, he moved deep into left field and stood next to the outfielder, both of them talking while the lumberyard scored twelve runs in their half of the first inning.

Will found what he thought was his beer between innings and sat down next to Felipe. Out past the outfield he could see Lisa's vehicle stopped in the middle of the road. Mundo, shirtless, his back tanned a deep brown, was crouched down by the passenger window. After a few seconds, he rose and backed away slowly, still talking. Will could just catch the motion of Lisa's hand waving from inside the car. She put the car in gear and swung around the field and parked beside his truck. He watched her climb out and get into Felipe's truck with Elena.

"Your friend's here," Felipe said.

"I see her."

Felipe took a swallow of beer. "Not that one," he said. "Back in the trees. Behind the backstop."

Lalo's car was parked in the woods. The vehicle sat so low that the grass reached up to the front bumper. Alongside it and parked close was Jimmy's truck. There were a couple of guys Will had never seen before between the two vehicles, watching the game and drinking. The windows of both vehicles were tinted so dark that Will couldn't make out anything inside. Maybe some shadows, like limbs moving.

"Who are those guys?" he asked.

"Ray's nephews. They're not from here. They were at the rosary. They'll be here until after the funeral."

"Doesn't Ray have any relatives who are girls?" Will said.

Felipe snorted and took another drink of beer. They watched Rudy hit a weak ground ball to Lawrence at first.

Rudy didn't even bother to run. He looked at Lawrence and dropped his bat and walked away mumbling.

"I didn't see those guys drive up," Will said. "How long have they been here?"

"When Albert was telling about the pig," Felipe said. "You know, Will, we have enough players. Maybe you should walk around the field and get your truck and go home."

Will didn't say anything for a few seconds. He thought he'd rather be here among so many people than at his house alone. "No," he said. "It's too nice an evening. Nothing's going to happen."

Rudy sat down heavily on the other side of Will. He whistled out some air as if he'd just sprinted a mile. Will looked back at Lalo's car. "This is a pretty small village," he said, "to be hiding from someone all the time."

"Hiding from who?" Rudy said. "Those guys? Fuck those guys. Just because you killed their uncle doesn't mean you have to worry." A gurgling sound that Will recognized as a laugh came out of Rudy's throat. He looked at the side of Rudy's face.

"I didn't kill their uncle," he said. "And I hope that damn pig had rabies."

Felipe stood in right field and watched the lumberyard hit the ball everywhere and then run around the bases like rabbits while his team fielded poorly and threw worse. He thought that not only was his team going to lose by an uncountable number of runs, but there was no game better than this one. What other game, he thought, allowed you to run sometimes and not at all at others.

You didn't have to knock anyone down, and every so often you got to hit a ball with a bat made out of wood. If you missed it, all that happened was you sat back down in the shade and popped open another can of beer. He watched Joe walk up to the plate and hit the ball hard on the ground to Juanito, who caught it by accident and then threw it in the dirt to Albert, who also caught it by accident and that was that.

Felipe and Will walked off the field together, and Felipe could see that Will, who took the game too seriously and ran after the ball everywhere, was tiring.

"This game is supposed to be fun," Will said.

"You run too much."

Will looked at Felipe. He noticed that even on such a warm evening, there wasn't a bead of sweat on Felipe's face. "What do you mean I run too much?" he said. "When the ball is hit over my head, I'm supposed to walk after it?"

"Yes," Felipe said. "You have to pace yourself."

Will didn't say anything. He shook his head and turned and picked through the bats as if one were different from another. He looked across the field and could see Elena and Lisa in the cab of Felipe's truck. The two of them were talking quickly and laughing. Will could hear the kids by the creek, and how loud their voices were, and he knew they were all soaked with water and were all throwing things. Octaviano and Joe's boy suddenly darted out from behind a parked vehicle and ran across the infield, and Joe, on the pitcher's mound, waved them off with his glove. Back in the woods, Jimmy and Lalo and Lalo's friend had gotten out of their vehicles and were standing with their two cousins, drinking and keeping their eyes only on Will.

Felipe watched Will walk up to the plate. Then he looked down at the ground between his legs. He thought that sometimes it was no good to think anymore about anything, that there were things you could do and things you couldn't, and that in the end there was only waiting. He moved the flat of his hand across the grass and wondered how with no rain the grass could feel damp on his skin. When he looked up, Will was in the batter's box saying something to Joe, and behind him, Ray Pacheco's nephews were walking together out of the shadows of the trees.

The sound of Lloyd yelping behind Will made him turn around, and that was when he got hit. The blow caught his shoulder and the side of his head and flung him forward onto his hands and knees in front of home plate. The bat was on the ground not far from his face, and he could read the words etched in the wood. He reached for it and saw Joe still on the mound. Their eyes met, and then all Will could see around him were legs. "Hey," he said in a whisper.

He tried to get up and saw a leg pull back. The kick struck him on the side below his ribs, and instead of rising with the blow, he felt himself cave in, his body curling up. The leg pulled back and kicked again, the toe of the boot hitting hard into Will's shoulder. Will tried to get back on his hands and knees, and someone on the other side of him swung his leg. A foot smacked the left side of Will's face and there was a popping noise in his neck and his face went numb. He kept trying to move forward, his hands sliding along the ground. Noises came out of his mouth as if they belonged to someone else. He actually made it to a crouch once and stumbled a few steps before he was tripped up and landed hard in the dirt. He didn't know how long it lasted. Five minutes, ten, forever. He got kicked endlessly, as though he weren't quite human anymore. Limbs banging off his skull, his spine, tearing at his face.

Will ended up on his butt, his right hand resting on third base. His index finger was bent at an awkward angle. The fingernail was half on and half off and rimmed in blood. The skin was scraped away from his forearm and not yet bleeding, as though his flesh had gone into shock and didn't know how to respond. His body felt pumped up and numb, and as he tried to breathe, a stream of blood ran from his face and stained the front of his shirt. I'm hurt, he thought, and then he felt a soft rush of panic.

He was suddenly grabbed from behind, under the arms, and pulled up enough that he backpedaled and fell on his butt. He hit hard again and flat, and the impact de-flated his lungs and sent shock waves through his ribs. He tried to speak and saw blood spray out of his mouth. Will felt himself panic again, and he heard Felipe's voice say, "Get up. Come on, Will, get up." When Felipe tried to

lift him once more, Will went with it and ended up standing, swaying, beside him.

Will turned his head and looked at Felipe. He could
see dirt on Felipe's face. "How bad is it?" Will asked, and
a drop of blood landed on Felipe's cheek.

"Squeeze your nose," Felipe said. "With your fingers.
Maybe it just looks bad."

Will brought his hand to his face, and when he
squeezed both nostrils tight, so much blood clogged the
back of his throat that he had to bend over and spit it out.
When he straightened back up he could feel the muscles
cramp across his chest.

Lisa was standing beside Joe, and in front of them,
Jimmy and Lalo and their cousins were moving around
like cattle that didn't want to be corralled. Elena ran past
home plate to Octaviano and Joe's son, who were hud-
dled close together. Octaviano was crying with his mouth
open and staring at Will as though Will were the thing
that lived under his bed. The right fielder inched his way
off the field toward the parked cars as if something embarrassing had happened and he thought it would be best
just to leave.

Lisa began yelling, or, Will thought, maybe she'd
been yelling all along. "You pigs. Doing this in front of
children. What kind of animals are you?"

"Get out of here, Lisa," Jimmy said, and Will wondered how his voice could be so calm. "This isn't any of
your business."

"When you do it in my face, it's my business," she

shouted at him. "When you do a thing like this in front of little children, it is. Five of you. Five of you to do this." She glanced at Will and then turned back to Jimmy. "I'm not moving from here, Jimmy."

Lalo walked up close to Joe and pointed his arm at Will. "I'll take him," he said. "Just me and him. I don't need anyone else."

Joe pushed lightly on Lalo's chest. "Give it up," he said. "It's all over now."

"He fucked up," Jimmy said to Lisa.

"So you don't fuck up?"

"You know what he did?"

"So he's stupid," Lisa said. "So what? He didn't deserve this. No one deserves this. When he gets better you can come and beat him up by yourself if that will make you feel good."

From beyond the outfield, Will could see Mundo's truck moving forward. He drove across center field, the truck picking up speed. He pulled up close and jumped out of the cab. He moved quickly past his sister and up to Jimmy. He shoved Jimmy hard in the chest with the flat of his hand. "Don't mess with my sister," he said. Jimmy said something in Spanish, and Mundo pushed him again and said, "Don't ever mess with my sister."

Jimmy and Mundo stared at each other for a few seconds until finally Jimmy's body sagged slightly and he turned to Lalo. "Let's go," he said. "We're done here."

Felipe helped Will walk off the field and eased him down in the shade. Lisa crouched in front of him. "You can let go of your nose now," she said. "Someone give me something." Will's team seemed to be all around, and everyone looked at each other helplessly until Rudy finally undid his bandage and handed it to Lisa. She poured beer on it and wiped Will's face gently. She looked up at Felipe, who was thinking that Will didn't even look like Will anymore. "Maybe it's not too bad," she said.

Felipe shrugged. "His nose is flatter," he said.

Lisa turned back to Will. "Let me see your teeth." Will opened his mouth, and Lisa cocked her head and looked in. "They're all there," she said. "That's good. Does this hurt?" She poked him hard in the side. Will grunted and felt a pain so intense he nearly fell over. "At least you can talk," she said and stood up. "You sit here for a second and we'll help you home."

Lisa went over to Elena and put her hands on the shoulders of the two kids. Will heard her say, "They were bad men, hijos, weren't they?" Vehicles began pulling out from where they were parked and driving off slowly. Joe and Felipe were talking together out on the field. A few guys walked over to Will and told him to make sure he got some X-rays. That maybe he had a rib through a lung. Or maybe a brain concussion. That he had been kicked like a dead dog. Rudy sat down next to him and spent a moment studying the blue puncture marks on his arm. Then, without looking at Will, he said, "We were going to rally that inning, too."

Fifteen

FELIPE AND LISA WALKED
alongside Will in silence as he limped home. Octaviano
ran ahead of them, kicking at the ground and sending up
small clouds of dust. The sun had dipped below the tops
of the cottonwoods, and although Will could see pockets
of sun through the leaves, the old road he and Felipe and
Lisa walked was shaded. The soft breeze on his face made
him want to sit down in the grass and close his eyes and
not have to make his body move.

Just after being helped off the field and after Lisa had
wiped the blood from his face, Will had felt a quiet sense
of joy. He had thought that it was something to live
through a thing like this. But not much later, when he felt
his body relax in pain, he realized that on this field so near
his house, something worse than he even knew had happened.

It seemed to Felipe that the walk to Will's house was
taking forever. It had been Elena's idea that Will should
walk home so his muscles would stay loose and not turn
to cement. She had driven home in Felipe's truck, and
now Felipe walked beside Will in much the same way he

had once walked with his grandfather after his grandfather's third stroke, which had turned the old man's legs into sticks and bent his back so that even standing was difficult. Felipe glanced over at Lisa, who was looking at the ground, and he wondered how it had come to be that the three of them were now uncomfortable in each other's company.

When they finally got to the turn to Will's house, Felipe yelled for Octaviano to come back. He looked at Will. "You going to be okay?" he asked.

"Yes," Will said, and Felipe could see that one side of Will's face was bruised and swollen. "I'll be all right."

"It's over now," Felipe said. "There's nothing to worry about."

"I know."

"Then I guess I'll go home. Where are the keys to your truck?"

"In it."

Felipe nodded his head slowly and then said, "Let me see your hand. No, not that one. The one with the crooked finger."

The three of them looked at Will's hand and how the middle joint on his index finger was knotted up, pushing the top part of the finger out at an angle.

"You going to leave it that way?" Felipe asked.

Will moved the joint a fraction of an inch. "I don't know," he said. What he did know was that he didn't want to think about anything right now. "Maybe if I soak it, it will slide back in place."

"Let me see it." Felipe took Will's hand, grabbed the

finger, and pulled the joint back into place with a popping noise. "There," he said.

Will dragged air into his lungs, which made his ribs hurt. He shook his hand to get rid of the burning sensation that ran up to his wrist. "How could you just do that?" he said.

"Thank you, Felipe," Lisa said, and she put her hand on Will's arm. "Let's go home."

Will undressed slowly in the bathroom. Steam from the hot water running in the tub had clouded up the mirror, which was, he thought, just as well. When he had first glanced in the mirror, he found that he looked like something that had lain on the highway for days.

He worked his pants off and felt a little better. The only real injuries he could see were a swelling around his knee, a few scrapes, but not much more than that. Things got worse when he pulled off his shirt. There were no cuts, but the flesh from his hips to just under his arms had become one massive bruise. He thought that his whole body would soon look like Rudy's arm.

The phone rang in the kitchen. Lisa answered it and he heard her say hello over and over loudly. After a long pause, she slammed the phone down. She came to the bathroom doorway and stood there looking at him. Then she closed her eyes and stayed like that for a long time.

When she opened them, she looked older to Will. Her face was drawn, and there was a dullness in her eyes.

"Sometimes," she said so softly that he could barely hear her words, "I know in my soul that you are not for me, Will." She stood there a little longer and then turned and walked away. Even with the noise of the water running, Will could hear her close the front door as she left the house.

Telesfor Ruiz once told Will that when he was a young man, the priest in this village was named Father Joseph. A large man of German descent, he had been priest in Guadalupe for as long as anyone could remember. One spring, after a harsh winter, Father Joseph asked the people to assist him in making repairs to the church, which had stood for nearly two hundred years. If work was not done soon, Father Joseph said, the church would collapse in on itself, and then mass would have to be held in the fields with the animals. Surely a thing no one in Guadalupe would wish for.

Although the church walls had been built thick and sturdy and layers upon layers of mud plaster had strengthened them, the foundation was only loose stones, and over the years the walls had buckled with the weight. The roof, too, leaked badly, and the latillas between the vigas on the high ceiling had become water stained and in places rotted. Inside the church was always the odor of old wood and dampness.

On the day work was to begin, many men came to help, and their wives and daughters also came with platters of food. The day, Telesfor had said, smelled of lilacs and beans and garlic. Immense buttresses of adobe were built at each corner of the church to hold the walls in place. Nichos were carved into them, and everything was covered with a plaster mixed with straw and sand so that the building looked as though it grew from the earth.

On the day work was to begin on the roof, Telesfor came to the church at dawn, and he and Father Joseph set the ladder against the eave. Telesfor began to remove the wood shingles, which were worn from decades of wind and moisture to the thickness of paper. Father Joseph, who had felt poorly since winter and had lost much weight, rested on the peak of the roof and looked out over the village.

When Telesfor had cleared a large area, he lay down to peer between the boards into the attic space below him. The sun shone through in many places, and the air inside was a maze of floating dust. Beneath that, lying on top of the church ceiling, were the white bones of three men. Telesfor called out, and Father Joseph came and knelt beside him. Both could see how these three men had once lain down together side by side and how their hands, which were now no more than gray sticks, rested upon each other. Scattered about them everywhere were the small skeletons of thousands of birds.

The day Telesfor Ruiz told him this story, Will had walked to Telesfor's house late in the day. He had been in Guadalupe only a few months and knew no one but his neighbor. Telesfor told him that evening that he now slept poorly at night and always dreamed. He said that he had grown so old that only those who were dead were in his dreams.

Will had asked Telesfor whether anyone in Guadalupe had known who the men in the church attic were or how they had come to be in such a place. Telesfor said that it was a story he only knew the end of and that one could think too much or not at all about such things.

When Elena woke in the morning, she was alone in bed, and she could hear Felipe talking on the phone in the next room. She lay there on her back with her legs sprawled out and her eyes half open, listening to her husband. When she heard him say, "Bueno. I'll see you in a few minutes," her eyes opened fully and she threw the blanket aside and got out of bed.

Felipe had just picked up his lunchbox and was about to leave for work when Elena walked into the kitchen. Her hair was not yet brushed and was tangled about her face from sleep. She was wearing a robe that covered little of her body, and Felipe's first thought when he saw her was that his wife was beautiful. The second thought came after he saw the expression on her face, and it was that he wished he had already left the house.

"Where are you going?" Elena asked him in a low voice so as to not wake her sleeping children.

"I'm going to work," Felipe said in a loud whisper. "Where else would I be going?"

"With who?"

Felipe opened and closed his mouth. It occurred to him that his wife had a way of always saying what she thought, and he wished, not for the first time, that she had been born mute. "Rudy's going to help me," he said finally.

"And what about Will? Have you talked to him about this?"

"Do you think he can even walk this morning?"

"You know that's not what I asked," Elena said, and she pulled the robe together, covering her breasts, which now made little difference to Felipe. "I asked if you talked to him."

"No," Felipe said. "I didn't want to disturb him," which was only half true. Felipe thought a conversation with Will after what had happened at the baseball field would be awkward and embarrassing and not something he wished to face this morning. He had planned on driving Will's truck back to his house quietly and then riding with Rudy to work, where he could forget about all this for a few hours.

"You and Will have worked a long time together for you to do this to him."

"Me?" Felipe said loudly, wondering how his wife could so easily and with only a few words drive him to the edge of a cliff. "I'm not doing anything."

"That's right," Elena said, "you're not. And if you wake the children . . ."

"All right. All right," Felipe said in a harsh whisper. "I'll drive his truck back and if he's up, I'll talk to him. If not, I'll look in his window and see if he's still breathing."

"Good," Elena said, and she smiled. "And after that, call me so Lisa doesn't worry all day."

"Lisa?"

Just after Felipe had come home the night before, Lisa had driven up in her small car and stormed into the house. Her eyes were red and her face was swollen, and beneath all that Felipe had seen an anger he thought could go anywhere. He had gone to bed immediately, leaving her and Elena in the kitchen drinking wine coolers. He had fallen asleep hearing Lisa's voice and was startled awake once when she threw her glass against the wall, which was also the wall beside his bed.

Felipe looked at his wife. There was a soft expression on her face now, and she was still smiling. "What does Lisa care?" he said. "She hates Will."

"So?" Elena said.

Will slept for thirty-six hours. He slept poorly in a state that was not quite sleep but only bordered it, getting out of bed just once. And even then, it took such effort merely to climb from the bed and he was in so much pain that he thought if he were to die, it would not be something that concerned him. He had made his way slowly to the kitchen and drunk from the tap. Then he had filled a small pot with water and dropped a cup into it. He had stood by the sink for a moment as if lost in his own house. Then he had taken the Lady from the wall and carried all these things back to his bedroom. He put the water on the floor beside the bed and stood the Lady on the windowsill. The room was dark, and when he finally eased back into bed, all he could see was the small figure standing by the open window.

In his mind, he told the Lady that he knew she was here to protect the health of this house and those who lived here and that she had done a rotten job of it. He told her that possibly his judgment had been poor the last few days, and while it was true he kept her in a hole in his wall where there were spiders, still he didn't feel that he should be beaten and kicked in front of the entire village for things like this. He said that he would give her one more chance. If she failed, he would use her for fire in the stove, where she wouldn't throw enough heat for a pot of coffee. Sometime later, Will dreamed that he woke and it was light. Two faces that looked a great deal like Felipe and Rudy were staring in the window at him, but when the Lady looked back at them, they left without speaking. Will remembered nothing else, and when he woke again, it was the next day, and although most of what he felt upon waking was pain, he was also starving.

He spent the morning eating. His face was still swollen, and his ribs and chest hurt if he breathed too deeply. The pain in his body was no longer feverish but had settled into a stiffness that made his movements slow and deliberate. The door to the house stood open, letting sun and a light breeze into the kitchen. Will had lost a day and he knew there were things he should be doing, but he couldn't think what they were. He sat at the table looking at the two empty plates that had held his breakfast: five eggs with chile, a half pound of bacon, two tortillas and three pieces of toast. He had eaten a little too much for his first meal in two days, and all he really wanted to do was go back to bed.

He walked to the doorway and lit a cigarette. He could see his truck parked not far from the house and realized that Felipe must have driven it over while he slept. The leaves of the cottonwood moved in the breeze, and it seemed to Will that their color was a soft shade lighter, as though even in July they had begun to think of autumn. He brought the cigarette to his mouth and took another shallow breath full of smoke.

Lisa would be waiting tables at the café. Will could see her, her face dark and her hair pulled loose in places. He wondered what was going on in her mind, and then he remembered her last words to him. He thought that his life had twisted to some other place in just a few days, and he no longer knew where he was. He dropped his cigarette and ground it out. He took a few steps away from the house and then kept on walking.

Telesfor Ruiz's house sat in weeds now. The windows were boarded up with plywood, and the door had been nailed shut from the inside. The shed where Telesfor's father had stored his wood and where the santos had once stood looking out over fields of snow had fallen in on itself. Where Telesfor had grown a small garden, there was only sagebrush and tall grass.

Will hadn't been here in years. He could see that most of the roofing paper had blown off the house. The rest was pitted and torn, and the exposed wooden slats were weathered gray and black and were warping free from the nails. Plaster had fallen away from the walls in large chunks. Will thought that Telesfor's house was crumbling from the outside, while inside there was no light and nothing changed.

Will walked under the portal, where there was shade, and lowered himself to the ground. He stretched out his legs and leaned against the wall. He could feel the adobe cool against his back. Foothills were all around him here, and rising above them were mountains. Dark spruce and aspen climbed the slopes. Will closed his eyes and leaned his head back. He thought that Telesfor had been dead for years and that he did not even know where the old man was buried or anything about his relatives, other than those who had come before him. It seemed to Will that all that was left of Telesfor Ruiz were whispers only he heard. He thought it was possible that all he had left now in Guadalupe were ghosts, and although that wasn't so bad, he knew it wasn't enough. It came to him that if he didn't leave this place, he might become lost here by himself.

Sixteen

✛

L ISA KNEW THAT IT
was at least noon, if not later, and that she shouldn't still
be in bed, a place she liked only to sleep or to be with
someone else. Not to lie there as she had since early
morning, sweating from the heat beneath her great-
grandmother's bedspread and thinking about things that
made her want to cry or go crazy. To make things worse,
her mother had knocked on the door earlier and yelled
out to her daughter that she had been too long alone in
her trailer. Lisa was too old to worry her mother like this,
she said, and besides, didn't she know when she'd been
blessed with good luck? This didn't make Lisa feel any
better. Lying in bed, she had closed her eyes and told her
mother not to worry and that she would come out soon.

Lisa's mother had never cared for Will. When they
were in each other's company, they seldom spoke, a
thing, Lisa knew, that was not Will's fault. But as soon as
he was gone, her mother would not shut up about him.
It seemed as if, from the moment her mother had learned
of Will's existence in Lisa's life, even the simplest words,

such as "How are you this morning, hija?" would some-how lead to Will.

Lisa's mother didn't like how Will was always so quiet around her, or how he looked at her daughter when he thought no one was watching. She also didn't like that when he walked into her house, he seemed too tall for the ceiling. She thought his truck was too old and ugly and made too much noise. She didn't like that the house he lived in had once belonged to Marcello Rael, whose cows had one night long ago escaped their pasture and roamed Guadalupe eating clothes that had been left out and tram-pling gardens and even killing a dog belonging to Fred Ramírez, a thing, Lisa's mother had said in a hushed voice, that cows were not known to do. She said that Will's name sounded flat in the mouth like a stone and that if she ever had a daughter whose name was Lisa Sawyer, she would die of shame. And besides all that, this man had no family.

Lisa would listen to these things while cooking with her mother or cleaning up around the house and think that she never had much luck with men. It didn't matter that this was often her own fault, it was still true. She knew in her heart that she had found something with Will, but she didn't know what it was. It bothered her that what she had found always seemed to do something stupid and probably always would, but she also knew that this was something she didn't want to lose.

Lisa flung off the blanket and sat up with her legs off the bed. In front of her on the floor was a mob of Saint Francises, and all of them looked back at her. For the first time, she realized that although it was true they were all saints, it was also true that they were all men who lived in her bedroom. It occurred to her that maybe she should be wearing more than what she had on, which was nothing, and then she thought that they had seen her this way for a long time. If they weren't used to it by now, it was their problem. She looked down at them and smiled.

"I think," she said with her breath, "we'll do something today." She swung her legs back and forth, thinking that first she would walk to her mother's house and have coffee. Then she would take a long, hot bath. She would not rush things, but do them slowly. She stood up and stretched, naked in the sun coming in the window.

"We've left him alone with himself for too long," she said out loud, "and who can tell what goes through his mind then?"

Will drove his truck through the village. Beside him on the seat was a brown paper bag, and in the bed of the pickup in plastic bags were most of his clothes and his bedding, his rifle, a few pots and pans, and some things that had once belonged to his father. The rest of his things he'd left in the house, not even caring whether he saw them again. He drove by Juan Martínez, who was on his tractor, and both of them automatically raised a hand. It was late afternoon and Will figured that after he was finished with what he was going to do, he'd drive south until he was too tired to go any farther and the next morning would keep on driving. He thought that the name *Guadalajara* had a nice sound to it, although he had no idea where it was. He knew it was south of here and that if he aimed his truck that way, anything could happen.

Will turned off the highway and onto the gravel road that would take him up the canyon. A little way up he saw Flavio Montoya, a man growing old, leaning against his shovel in the middle of his alfalfa field. He was wearing a baseball cap and rubber boots that were muddy and came to his knees. As Will drove by, Flavio, without looking at him, raised his chin in a wave. Felipe had once told Will that a long time ago, Flavio Montoya's dead grandparents had come back to haunt him because as a child, Flavio had killed his grandmother's favorite chicken. At the time, Will had nodded his head and smiled and said nothing because he thought anything else Felipe might say would lead to a place that made even less sense. Now he thought it was possible the entire village was touched with a strain of insanity and that even if it weren't, who would want to live somewhere where people came back from the dead because of a chicken?

A mile later, Will came to the faded red flatbed abandoned at the end of Ray Pacheco's drive. He downshifted and then stopped at the entrance. He could see Ray's house a quarter of a mile off the road. The only vehicle parked in front of it was Ray's pickup. Will took a cigarette out of his shirt pocket and lit it. Then, trying not to think about what he was doing, he swung off the road and drove to Ray's house.

A small girl came to the door. She didn't open it but stood just inside the house staring out at Will through the screen. Her hair was long and black and brushed smooth, and her skin was dark. All Will could really see of her face was eyes. She wore a white dress that had pictures of baby animals stenciled all over it. On her shoulder, Will could see an animal that looked like something he had never seen before.

"Is your tía home?" he asked.

"Why is your face like that?"

"Because I fell on it," Will said. He looked past her into the house. A small boy sat in front of a television set against the far wall. There was carpet on the floor and wood paneling on the walls, and the curtains were drawn so that the room was shadowed. Will looked back down at the girl, who was still staring up at him. "Is that your brother in there?" he asked.

She nodded. "He falls on his face too," she said. "All the time. But not in bed. But sometimes he falls out of the bed. He forgets to watch his feet." Will suddenly felt that coming here was a bad idea and that he would spend forever on weak legs talking about feet and faces.

"If you watch your feet," he said, "then you can't see where you're going."

"My brother never knows where he's going," she said, and it occurred to Will that if Lisa were to have a sister she would be like this. "Did you fall on a rock?" she asked.

"No," Will said. "I fell on somebody's foot." Probably your father's, he thought. "So, is your tía here?"

"My Tía Josepha is, but Tía Bella went to the church." She looked down at the paper bag Will had carried with him from the truck. "Have you brought food?"

"No," Will said.

"Do you want to come in?"

"Yes," he said.

Will followed the girl through the house, and even before he reached the kitchen, he could smell the heavy aroma of food. Chile and cilantro and honey. The kitchen counters were jammed with flat pans of enchiladas and chile rellenos. There were pots of beans and menudo and plates stacked high with tortillas and sopapillas. On the windowsill above the sink were vases of flowers, and in the middle of them was a large photograph of Ray. He was wearing a suit and not smiling, and he seemed out of place on the windowsill among so many flowers.

At a small table in the room sat a woman so old that Will wondered if she were breathing. Her back was curved so much that although her chair was pushed a few feet from the table, her head rested just above the table-top. Her hair was white and thin with age, but her face was smooth and pale. To Will, she seemed like someone who had stepped past life, and he felt that if she were to speak, it would be in words he would not understand. On the table before her was a plate of food that had gone untouched.

The young girl stood in front of Will and said loudly, "This man came to see you, Tía Josepha."

The old woman raised only her eyes and looked at

Will. "Sientate," she said with just her breath, and Will could see that her head was trembling slightly.

"I came to see Ray's wife," Will said.

"She's at the church, I told you," the girl said. "Tía, his face is like that because he fell."

"Va a su hermano," the woman said in a voice that was stronger, and the girl walked around Will and out of the room. "Sientate," she said again.

Will stood in the doorway. The sun shone through the window, and the light was full of the odor of garlic and flowers. After a moment, he walked to the table, pulled out a chair, and sat down.

"Mi hijo es muerte," Josepha said. Sitting this close to her, Will could see that her face was woven with fine wrinkles and that her eyebrows were no more than a white shadow. She brought her hand from her lap and placed it on Will's. Her fingers were swollen and knotted at the knuckles. "Mi hijo es muerte . . . at the river." She spoke the words slowly and just above a whisper, and her eyes were clear, as though trapped in her body.

"Yes," Will said. "I know." He thought that he was sitting in Ray's kitchen with his mother and that of all the things that had happened, this might be the strangest. This would be something he would remember for a long time.

"Mi hijo was a good boy," Josepha said.

"Yes," Will said again.

"And did you see how young he looked in his death? Like a young man, my son looked."

"I saw."

"Pero," she said and looked down at the table. "Pero," she said again, and Will knew that she had become lost somewhere. Her head bobbed quickly up and down. She moved her hand to the plate of food before her and slid it a few inches toward Will. "Come," she said.

"No," Will said. "No thank you."

"Quiere agua?"

"No. I'm fine." He reached for the bag on the floor and said, "I've brought you . . ."

"When mi hijo was young," Josepha said, "he would not wear clothes." She raised her head ever so slightly and looked at Will. "Did you know this about my son?"

Will, who did not know what to say, said nothing. Not only couldn't he see Ray as a young boy, but he found it impossible to see Ray as a young boy without clothes.

"It's true," she went on, "he liked to wear nothing. And if it hadn't been for the hailstorm God sent, I think he would be doing it to this day. Every morning, but not in winter, mi hijo would go outside and take off his clothes and bury them in a hole. I would look from the window and see my son running through our fields naked with a large stick in his hands, as if chasing something. Sometimes he would run across the neighbor's field and the fields beyond that. This was not a thing his father, who always wore his clothes, even in bed, was proud of. And his sisters would cry in embarrassment and throw rocks at him. Every night I would pray to God that my

son would come to his senses, and finally God sent a hailstorm one summer afternoon in which even chickens
were struck dead where they stood."

"What happened to him in the hailstorm?" Will
asked.

"What do you think happened to him?" Josepha
replied. "My son wore clothes from that day on. Sometimes too many clothes. And for years, after a heavy rain,
one of mi hijo's shirts or a pair of his pants or a stocking
would wash out from below the ground."

Josepha stopped talking and dropped her eyes. Will
could see how thin her bare arms were. There seemed to
be little left of her inside her dress. He could see how
badly her head trembled, and he wondered that she was
able to talk for so long in a voice that had been so clear
and steady.

"Mi hijo was sick," she said. "Did you know that?"

"Yes," Will said. "I knew."

"And like an animal, that sickness caught my son at
the river."

Will saw the birds lift slowly off Ray's body. They settled in the sagebrush and stood there waiting. He
thought that an animal had caught them both at the river.

"I can see my son in my eyes. And he is little and he
is a man. I see him running to me when he would fall and
be hurt and crying. I see him through his whole life."

Will could not stay in this room any longer. There
was not a thing he could say, and he found it unbearable
to listen anymore. He picked up the bag and put it on his

lap. Then he reached inside and took out the santo of Our Lady of Guadalupe. He stood her in the center of the table. "I've brought you this," he said.

Josepha raised her eyes and gave out a small gasp. She stretched her hands out slowly and drew the Lady to her. "Mi hijo es muerte," she said in a whisper. She didn't say it to Will but to the Lady, and then she began to weep without tears.

When Will stood and turned he saw Ray's wife, Bella, standing just inside the kitchen. She was motionless and staring at him. "Why are you in my house?" she said.

"My name's Will Sawyer."

"I know who you are," she said. "Get out of my house."

Will walked by her. He could hear her footsteps as she followed him. The television was still on in the living room, and the two children sat before it.

"Be careful of your feet," the young girl said to him.

"I will," Will answered.

"Tía, his face is like that because . . ."

"Hush, hija," Bella said.

Will walked out the door and onto the porch. The sun had set below the hills, and the clouds and the mountains to the east were burnt red. The alfalfa in the fields was dark green and thick, and for a second, Will thought he could actually smell it.

Bella stood behind him, inside the door, and to his back she asked, "What have you done with the photographs?"

As he looked out at the fields, Will could see the photographs of the girl in the wall of his kitchen. "I burned them," he said and took a step away from the house.

"My husband never knew what happened to that girl."

Will turned around. Through the screen he could see only her shadow.

"Do you know what I'm saying?" she asked.

"No."

"I'm saying that whatever you came here for, you could never find. And that all of this has been for nothing. Now go."

When Will drove past the baseball field and swung into his drive, he saw Felipe's truck coming toward him from his own house. They stopped alongside each other.

"Hey," Will said.

"Hey yourself."

Neither of them spoke for a few seconds and then Will said, "Come on back. We'll drink a beer."

Felipe looked at him. He had just been inside Will's house, and what he had seen there, he didn't want to see again. He especially didn't want to see it again with Will beside him. He knew that Will would not be drinking any beer this evening.

"No," he said. "I just came by to make sure you were still alive."

"I'm still breathing," Will said.

"You don't look so bad."

"That's because it's almost dark."

Felipe nodded. He pushed the shift into gear and left his foot on the clutch. "I answered the phone when I was in your house," he said. "It was Monica. She said tomorrow it was going to rain, and if her baby drowns, it will be your fault."

"Her roof leaks," Will said.

"I'll come by in the morning. We'll go fix it." Felipe let the truck roll a little, and Will could see him grinning inside the cab. "Good luck, jodido," he said and drove off.

When Will walked up to his house, the door swung open, and standing there was Lisa. She was wearing her great-grandmother's wedding dress and it was tight, tight on her body. The lace collar around her neck was buttoned, and the hem of the dress came far above her knees. Will could smell the odor of mothballs. He thought she looked like a deranged ballerina. He also thought that Lisa's great-grandmother must have been a dwarf.

"I knew you would come back," she said, moving her hands over the front of her dress. "You know what this means?"

"It means you want to marry me."

"Or maybe I just got married to someone else. Did you ever think of that?"

"Is that what you did?"

"No," she said. "That's not what I did." They stood for a few seconds looking at each other. Finally, she said, "If you walk through this door, you can't leave again. Do you understand?"

"This is my house," he said.

"That's no answer."

"Yes," Will said. "I understand."

"That's what makes me mad with you. You say yes, but you don't think. Listen to me one more time, and I will say it again. If you walk through this door, you will stay here forever, and if things go bad, and they will because of what you are, I'll have to shoot you."

"You'll kill me if we have problems?"

She nodded slowly. Her mouth was open slightly, and Will could see the tip of her tongue. "Or maybe I'll just wound you," she said.

"Does this mean that if we have children, Mundo will be their uncle?"

Lisa smiled and looked away. "Tío Mundo," she said. "He'll be so proud."

Will looked past her into his house. He could see that standing on his kitchen table and crowded together on the floor was an army of Saint Francises. Some of them were smiling and some weren't, and they all looked a little uneasy in his house. Will thought that each one of them was looking straight at him, waiting to see what he would do.